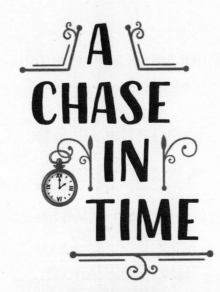

A CHASE IN TIME

SALLY NICHOLLS

OTHER BOOKS BY THIS AUTHOR

WAYS TO LIVE FOREVER

AN ISLAND OF OUR OWN

THINGS A BRIGHT
GIRL CAN DO

MAKE MORE NOISE!
(CONTRIBUTOR)

To my Auntie Jean,
with thanks for
all the summers.

First published in the UK in 2018 by Nosy Crow Ltd

This edition published in 2020

The Crow's Nest, 14 Baden Place
Crosby Row, London, SE1 1YW

Nosy Crow and associated logos are trademarks and/or registered
trademarks of Nosy Crow Ltd.

ISBN: 978 1 78800 866 2

A CIP catalogue record for this book is available from the British Library.

Printed and bound in Great Britain by Clays Ltd, Elcograf S.p.A.

Papers used by Nosy Crow are made from wood grown in sustainable forests.

MIX
Paper from
responsible sources
FSC® C018072

1 3 5 7 9 10 8 6 4 2

www.nosycrow.com

CHAPTER ONE
THE BOY IN
THE MIRROR

The mirror hung by the stairs in Aunt Joanna's hallway. It was tall and wide, with a gold frame full of curling leaves, and scrolls, and fat baby angels, and baskets of flowers, and twiddles. Aunt Joanna said it had once belonged to a French aristocrat, in the days before the revolutionaries chopped off all the aristocrats' heads and turned their palaces into art galleries.

And once, when Alex Pilgrim was seven years old, he had looked into the mirror and another boy had looked back.

The boy in the mirror was Alex's age, or perhaps a little older. He had light-brown hair and a sturdy sort of face. He was wearing a woolly blue jumper and grey knickerbockers. Knickerbockers, if you don't know, are an old-fashioned type of trouser – shorter than long trousers but longer than shorts – worn by old-fashioned schoolboys in the days before boys were allowed real trousers.

This boy was brushing his hair in the mirror,

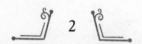

rather hurriedly, as though he would much rather be doing something else. As Alex watched, he turned his head sideways and yelled at somebody out of sight. Alex couldn't hear what he said, but it sounded impatient: "I'm doing it!" perhaps, or "I'm coming!" Then he put the hairbrush down and ran out of the frame.

Alex stayed by the mirror. It still showed Aunt Joanna's hallway, but nothing in the hallway was quite as it ought to be. The walls were papered with yellow-and-green-striped wallpaper, and there was a large green plant he had never seen before and a white front door with coloured glass above the sill. It felt very strange not to see his own face looking back at him. He put out a hand,

and there was a sort of ripple in the reflection. When the picture settled, there he was as usual: small, fair-haired, and rather worried-looking. There was the ordinary cream wall behind him. There was the ordinary brown door. Everything just as it always was.

Alex had never believed in those children in books who discovered secret passageways, or Magic Faraway Trees, or aliens at the bottom of the garden, and kept them a secret. Wouldn't you want to tell everyone about them? What was the fun of a secret passage if you had no one to boast about it to?

But he knew that he would never tell his family about the boy in the mirror. Of course he wouldn't.

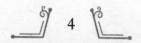

What would be the point? None of them would ever believe him.

After he saw the boy, though, the mirror became Alex's favourite thing at Applecott House. He liked it more than the long garden with the high stone walls, and the blackberry bushes, and the apple trees. He liked it more than the three cats, and the rabbit in the hutch, and the playroom with the doll's house, and the rocking horse, and the ship in the bottle, and the shelves of old-fashioned children's books.

Alex loved beautiful things. He, his sister Ruby, and their parents lived in a scrubby little house on a scrubby little estate on the edge of an ugly

red-brick town. Aunt Joanna's house was about as different from Alex's house as it was possible for an English house to be. It was big and old and rather grand – it always made Alex think of William's house in the *Just William* books. It had iron gates with a stone ball on the top of each gatepost, and two staircases – a grand one for family and a poky one for the servants. Not that Aunt Joanna had any servants nowadays, of course. Nowadays, she ran a bed-and-breakfast business, and all the bedrooms were kept nice for bed-and-breakfast guests.

Aunt Joanna was really Ruby and Alex's father's aunt. Both of their parents worked busy jobs, which was OK most of the time but made school holidays complicated. Ever since they were small, Ruby and Alex had gone to stay with Aunt Joanna for two weeks on their own every summer. Their parents paid for their bedroom, like proper bed-and-breakfast guests, and every evening they had to write on a piece of paper whether they wanted sausages or eggs or bacon for breakfast. They would help Aunt Joanna with the bed-and-breakfast work as well. Ruby's favourite job was polishing the breakfast table, by sitting on the duster and skidding around on top of it. Alex's was folding the bed sheets, Aunt Joanna on one side, him and Ruby on the other, the three of them coming to meet in the middle.

Applecott House was full of lovely objects. Aunt

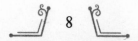

Joanna's great-uncle had travelled all around the world collecting things, and most of the things he had collected had ended up in Applecott House. There were jade and ebony cabinets from Japan, statues of gods from ancient Peru, and brightly coloured vases and plates from Turkey. Alex loved them all. But he loved the mirror best.

"Is it very old?" he asked Aunt Joanna, the summer he was ten and Ruby was twelve. "A hundred years old? Five hundred? A thousand?"

"Probably about two hundred and fifty," she said. "It's lovely, isn't it? But I expect it'll have to go when the house is sold."

Because this was the last holiday Alex and Ruby would spend with Aunt Joanna. At the end of the

summer, the house was to be sold and most of the lovely objects with it. Aunt Joanna would go and live in a little flat in Eastcombe, by the sea, where there would be no room for beautiful French mirrors or inlaid cabinets from Japan.

Everyone was very sorry about this. Alex minded so much about Applecott House being sold that it hurt. But even he didn't mind as much as Aunt Joanna did. Aunt Joanna had been born in Applecott House. It was Aunt Joanna who had worked so hard to keep it. She had set up the bed-and-breakfast business, and done all the cooking and cleaning and washing and accounting, just so the house didn't have to be sold. But at last, she had had to admit defeat. She was getting too old to do the work. And the house got more expensive to look after every year. Pipes kept bursting, and tiles kept falling off the roof, and mysterious things kept going wrong with the central heating.

"Ah, well," she said to Alex, as he helped to water the garden. "I suppose it had to happen some day. Still, it's a wrench, after all these years."

"I wish I had millions and millions of pounds," Alex said to Ruby that afternoon, as they sat in the garden. Ruby was reading. Alex was playing with a silver bottle he'd found in one of the cabinets. It had a round silver stopper, which he was trying to unscrew, but it didn't want to come out. "I'd buy Applecott House and let Aunt Joanna live here as long as she wanted."

"I wouldn't," said Ruby. "I'd buy a castle in France, with a swimming pool, and a private cinema, and a butler who did everything I asked him to, including homework, and an enormous library like Belle's in *Beauty and the Beast*, and a garden so big I could hold rock festivals in it, and…"

But Alex didn't care about any of those things.

"I want Aunt Joanna not to have to sell the house," he said. "That's all I want."

As he said the words, the stopper came out of the bottle, so suddenly that he dropped the whole thing in surprise. A great quantity of dust and smoke poured out on to his lap.

Ruby said, "Eugh! What is it?"

"I don't know," said Alex. He tipped the bottle upside down, sending another cloud of dust mushrooming out.

Ruby coughed and waved her hands, and said, "I hope that's not something important! What is it, someone's ashes?"

"I don't think so," said Alex. He looked down into the bottle. There didn't seem to be anything else inside. "Not a person's ashes. It might be a hamster's."

"It's old, anyway," said Ruby. She took the bottle from him and frowned. "Yuck! Why don't we ever get a bottle with a genie in it?"

"It'd be my genie if we did," said Alex.

The rest of the day passed the way days at Applecott House always passed. They walked into the village and bought sweets at the Co-op. They picked blackberries from the garden and made a summer pudding for tea. They played a long game of Monopoly that ended, as usual, with Ruby owning half the board, and Alex nothing but two pound notes.

"To buy a cup of tea with," said Ruby. "I'm charitable, me. I give to the homeless."

"Huh," said Alex.

It wasn't until they were going up to bed that he remembered the bottle. There it sat, on the hall table. He picked it up, feeling vaguely guilty.

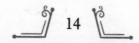

Perhaps that dust *had* been something important.

"I wish you really were a genie," he said sadly. Then he looked in the mirror, just in case there were any ghosts there tonight.

And there were.

In the mirror were two children. One was the same boy Alex had seen three years ago. Alex had grown, but the boy had stayed exactly the same age, only this time he was wearing a sailor suit and holding a paper bag. An older girl was standing beside him. The girl, who looked about thirteen, had long dark hair and a rabbity sort of face. She was wearing a blue dress, black stockings and a white pinafore. She was trying to take something from the paper bag – Alex guessed it must have sweets in it – and the boy was trying to stop her.

"Ruby," said Alex, very cautiously. "Can you come over here? Like, now?"

"What is it?" said Ruby. Then she looked in the mirror. "*Whoa*."

"You *can* see them," said Alex. He'd been wondering if the whole thing might be a dream.

"Is it projecting from somewhere?" said Ruby. She looked around for a projector, but there wasn't one. "Maybe it's a TV screen," she said. "Is Aunt Joanna doing it? Do you think it's to help sell the house?"

"I don't think it's a TV," said Alex. But he started to feel worried. Could Ruby be right? Could the one magic thing that had ever happened to him be something ordinary after all? "Look," he said, and he touched the glass.

Except that there wasn't any glass any more. His hand went right through the mirror. Ruby squealed.

"Alex!"

Alex tried to pull his arm back, but found that he couldn't. It was like falling downhill in slow motion, except he was falling inside the mirror. He had to step forward to stop himself from tipping over. Ruby said, "Alex!" again, and then, "Alex, what's *happening*?"

"I don't know—" Alex said, and landed with a thump on his hands and knees.

"Ow!" said Ruby, behind him.

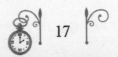

Someone screamed.

Alex looked up. He was on the floor in Aunt Joanna's hall, but everything was different. There was yellow-and-green-striped wallpaper, and a white front door with coloured glass above it, and all the furniture was wrong. Standing in front of him were two children, who were both screaming. One was a girl with a rabbity sort of face, and long, dark hair with a white ribbon in it.

The other was a boy in a sailor suit.

CHAPTER TWO
THE HOUSE BEHIND THE MIRROR

"Oh!" said Ruby. She scrambled up. "What just *happened*? And *stop screaming*!"

The boy and the girl stopped screaming. The boy scrambled backwards, so he was pressed as close to the girl as he could get. The girl put her

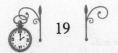

arm around him. They both looked terrified.

"Are you witches?" said the girl.

"No," said Alex. "I'm a boy, I'd be a wizard. But I'm just a boy. Where are we?"

"England," said the boy. He looked about eight. He seemed reassured by Alex's lack of wizardliness. "Suffolk. Dalton. Applecott House. I say, though – you *can't* just be an ordinary boy. You walked right out of a looking glass. Did you come from Looking-Glass Land, like in *Alice*?"

"The mirror!" said Alex. He looked around and, sure enough, there it was, hanging exactly where it had always hung in Aunt Joanna's house. It looked perfectly ordinary. It showed the new, strange hall, with the green-and-yellow wallpaper, and the four children. Alex went over to it and pressed his hand against the glass. It was just glass. Wherever they were now, they were stuck.

"I think—" he said, but no one was listening.

"We're in the past," Ruby was saying. "We've travelled in time! Why else would you all be wearing clothes like that? Unless it's a trick. Or a secret room or something – but it would have to be a pretty big one."

"It's a dream," the girl was saying. "I'm dreaming. Or I got knocked on the head, and I'm seeing things. Or—"

The little boy was hammering on the mirror.

"Let me through!" he was yelling. "Open Sesame, you beastly object! I want to go to Looking-Glass

Land!" He swung the mirror sideways, as though – like Ruby – he expected to find a secret door hidden behind it.

Alex said, "Don't!" at the same time as the girl cried, "Henry, you goop! You'll break it, and they'll never get back!"

"Everybody shut up right now!" Ruby yelled. They all stopped talking, rather shocked. "Right." Ruby pointed at the girl. "You. What's your name, and what date is it?"

"Dora," said the girl. "Dora Pilgrim. And this is my brother Henry. And it's the twenty-third of August, 1912."

"I knew it!" said Ruby. "I'm Ruby, and that's Alex. We've come from the future – from over a

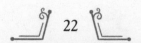

hundred years in the future. We're Pilgrims too – you must be our great-great-grandparents or something." Dora and Henry both started trying to argue, but she ignored them. "Henry might be. Your children would have a different surname, wouldn't they? Shut up, both of you! I can prove it – look."

She took her phone out of her jeans pocket and showed it to Dora and Henry.

"No signal," she said. She laughed, a little hysterically. "There wouldn't be, would there? But look!"

She flicked through her phone, searching – Alex supposed – for something spectacularly futuristic, which would prove they really did come from the twenty-first century. She settled on a video of Alex playing with one of Aunt Joanna's cats in the garden at Applecott House. It didn't look particularly futuristic to Alex, but Dora and Henry were impressed.

"It's like a Picture Palace in your pocket!" said Henry.

"But it's colour," said Dora. "It's better than the Picture Palace. And that's the garden here – isn't it? But everything's different. And you're different too. You smell different. And Ruby's a girl's name. You *are* a girl, aren't you? Do all girls wear trousers where you come from?"

"Who cares about trousers?" said Henry. "Do you all have time machines? Do people have wings yet?"

Dora and Henry did look different, Alex realised. Less *clean*. Their hair looked like it hadn't been washed in a week. Perhaps it hadn't. And they smelled, a bit, or Dora did at least. Perhaps deodorant hadn't been invented in 1912 either. There was an ingrained sort of grubbiness about them too. Henry had dirt under his fingernails, and grass stains on the knees of his knickerbockers. There was a sort of grubbiness to the whole house, actually. There was a heavy, lingering smell of coal smoke and a sharp, thick sort of smell which it took Alex a moment to realise was tobacco, as well as the ordinary country smells of grass, and flowers, and heavy summer air from the open

window. At least the garden smelled the same as it always did.

"*Well*—" he said.

Just then, the front door opened. Two men came through, carrying a wooden packing case, followed by a boy in a flat cap with a smaller box in his arms. One man looked like a servant; he also wore a flat cap, and hobnailed boots, but the other was young and wore a grey flannel suit and a grey hat, the sort with a brim and crease in the top.

"That's right," he was saying, "just through there – oh, hullo, kiddies! You couldn't grab that door for me, could you, old chap?"

"Old chap" seemed to be Henry, who ran over and opened the door to the living room. The men carried the packing case through. Alex and Ruby followed them curiously. The living room looked much less old-fashioned than Alex had expected. He'd thought perhaps it would look like a room on one of the period dramas his parents liked to watch, but it was much more lived-in. There were books and piles of paper on the table, which there never were in period dramas, and a heap of toys by the corner cupboard: a cricket ball and stumps, a couple of tennis racquets, a game of Snakes and Ladders and a draughts set, looking rather as though they'd been pulled out of the cupboard and abandoned. Alex had never thought that people in the past might be untidy. In his head, they all lived in neat, perfect, National Trust houses, except the poor people, who lived in thatched cottages, or slums. The Snakes and Ladders box was coloured in bright reds and blues, which was also unexpected. Alex had seen quite a lot of old-fashioned toys at museums and things, and they were almost always creased and faded and falling to bits. He supposed that was because they were old, and of course they must all have been new once. But it was still strange to see the old-fashioned box looking as bright and new as something you might buy in a toy shop.

Mostly, however, the living room was full of packing cases, piled two or three high in all the available floor space.

"Just sling it by the fireplace, Frank," the young man was saying. "Thanks awfully. Will you two be all right with the other one? I—"

"Atherton!"

The man jumped. A woman had appeared from somewhere and was standing in the doorway. She was wearing a long, dark-green dress, and black boots, and her brown hair was done up in a complicated hairstyle on top of her head. She was watching the man, who must be Atherton, with a mixture of exasperation and amusement.

Atherton looked guilty.

"Hello, Mary dear," he said. "Look what's arrived! It's the shrunken heads, I'm almost sure it is, and if it isn't, it's probably the amulets of power. Dora, my love, be a lamb and pass me that crowbar, would you? Just there, by the totem pole."

"*Atherton!*" said Mary. "I'm very pleased the shrunken heads have arrived, although really, I *don't* see why we have to keep all these things in the sitting room. But where on earth have you *been*? I haven't seen you since yesterday morning! It's not that I *mind*, exactly, but we've got a hall that needs decorating, and all the tables and things to lay out for tomorrow, and a girl does worry. You might have been *eaten*, or run over by a bus, or *anything*."

"Not *eaten*, my angel, not in Suffolk," said Atherton. "It was the queerest thing," he went on. "I just went into town to say cheerio to Charlie Higgins from school – frightfully good chap, he's off to India, you know, really thought I'd better say goodbye – *anyway*, Charlie said his old man had a sort of Saxon thing he was trying to get shot of, and would I like a squint at it? Well, once he'd told me what it was, I couldn't very well say no, could I? So I thought I'd just pop down—"

"Leaving me to deal with all your hideous relations on my own," said Mary. "Present company excepted, of course. And—"

"That's Uncle Atherton," Dora said, in a low voice to Alex and Ruby. "He went off to Peru last year to look for antiquities – he's going to start an antiquity exhibition and tour the country with it. It all started when he went to Mexico and found the most gorgeous hoard of Aztec treasure. It was worth simply heaps of money, and now he's spending it all on buying things for his exhibition. That's Miss Flynn. She's a lady anthropologist and he met her in the middle of a jungle. They kept having fights about whether buying artefacts from the natives was exploitation, or just trade. She made Uncle Atherton pay three times as much as he was going to for everything. And then he and Miss Flynn decided, since they enjoyed fighting each other so much, they might as well get married and do it in comfort. The wedding's tomorrow. Everyone's in the church hall putting up bunting right now."

The man and the boy had come back with another packing case. The boy bumped against Ruby as he passed. Alex was almost sure he did it deliberately.

"Scuse me, sir," he said, with a smirk.

"I'm a *girl*!" said Ruby. "And get your hands off me!"

Atherton and Mary, who were beginning what looked like a proper row, stopped arguing immediately and looked around.

"Who are your friends, Dora?" said Atherton. "I don't think we've been introduced. And why – if it's not an impertinent question – are they wearing fancy dress?"

"They're from the future!" said Henry, before Alex could stop him. "That mirror you gave Miss Flynn – it's a time machine!"

Atherton pulled what Alex and Ruby called a playing-with-the-children face.

"A *time machine*!" he said. "Crikey! You'd better not get too close, Mary, you'll get whisked off to prehistoric Britain. And knowing you, you'll start investigating their hunting rituals and never come back. And where would I be then?"

"Ass," said Mary affectionately. "You'd have

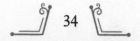

34

to come in after me. You'd make a very fetching prehistoric Briton, all in woad and fur."

"So I would," agreed Atherton cheerfully. "And so would you too. I've got a necklace of saber-toothed-tiger teeth somewhere that would suit you admirably. Thanks, Hodges, that'll do."

The man and the boy nodded, and went out.

"But they really *are* from the future!" said Henry, who'd been listening to all this with impatience.

"Not now, kiddos," said Atherton. He took the crowbar and began levering the lid off the smaller box the boy had been carrying. "We don't have time for games. Not with all my hideous relations here for the mating ritual – sorry, darling, I mean the happiest day of my life. And anyway, you haven't seen my artefact yet. What's inside this box is going to be the centrepiece of my exhibition. I *believe* it's the biggest chunk of Saxon gold ever discovered. The Newberry Cup – you've heard of it, Mary, of course?"

"Of course," said Mary. "You don't mean to say you've actually bought the Newberry Cup, do you? Why on earth didn't you say so at once?"

"Couldn't get a word in edgeways, I expect," said Atherton. "Mary, my angel, would you—"

"Here," said Mary. She took the box and held it as Atherton prised off the lid. The children crowded forward. Alex felt a quiver of anticipation. He could see that Atherton, like himself and Aunt Joanna, loved beautiful things. And anything that made him this excited must be a very beautiful thing indeed.

But before Atherton could so much as touch the straw that filled the box, a new person appeared in the doorway. A youngish-looking person in an apron, holding a mop.

"Mr Pilgrim, sir," she said. "You're to come at once! Something dreadful's happened!"

CHAPTER THREE
SOMETHING DREADFUL, AND SOMETHING MORE DREADFUL AGAIN

There was a moment's silence. Then Mary laughed.

"Is all this excitement usual, Atherton?" she said. Atherton looked a little indignant, then rather shamefaced. Then he laughed too.

"It is, rather," he said. "I say, though! You didn't want a quiet life, did you?" He turned to the woman with the mop. "Well?" he said. "Tell us the worst. Rats eaten the wedding cake? Archbishop of Canterbury forbidding the banns? Or just my dreadful relations causing their usual havoc?"

"No, sir!" said the maid (she must be a maid, Alex thought, with that mop). "The stables are on fire!"

"Great Scott!" said Atherton. He bolted out of the room, into the hall, and through the door that led to the kitchen. The others followed. The back door was open, and through it Alex could see billows of black smoke rising from somewhere at the bottom of the garden.

Atherton looked around him rather wildly and swore, a surprisingly modern-sounding swear word.

"Henry!" he said. "Run down to the village hall, can't you? Tell everyone to come back up here and help! Eileen!" (Eileen must be the maid.) "Call the fire brigade! And tell Cook and Hodges! You!" (He turned to Alex and Ruby.) "I don't know who you are, but you'd better make yourselves useful. Come on!"

He ran back into the hall and grabbed his hat from the hall sideboard (hats were evidently one of life's essentials, because Dora and Henry were also grabbing theirs from the hatstand by the door). Then they all went haring down the garden. Mary, Alex and Ruby followed.

The black smoke was coming from a long, low stone building at the bottom of the garden. The man in the flat cap who'd brought the crate in earlier – hadn't Atherton called him Hodges? – was frantically unwinding a hosepipe, which was attached to an old-fashioned handpump, of the sort with a lever that you worked up and down.

Ruby cried, "Oh, what about the horses?"

Alex had been wondering about them too. A stable had to have horses, didn't it?

"It's all right," said Dora. "They're down in the lower field."

Mary was calling out orders.

"Buckets! Hodges, let me do that. Atherton, for

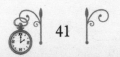

heaven's sake, start pumping. Hodges, you and the children, get as many buckets as you can."

"And fire brooms!" said Atherton. "On the back wall! Go on! Look slippy about it!"

Hodges dropped the hosepipe and stumbled off in the direction of the back wall. Alex ran after him. The brooms were easy enough to spot – three or four of them, neatly stacked against the wall. He and Hodges gathered them up and pelted back to the front of the stable. Mary had the hose unwound and was pointing it at the blaze;

Atherton, his sleeves rolled up and a streak of soot already splashed across his face, was working furiously at the handpump.

From another building across the yard, Dora and Ruby appeared, carrying three metal buckets.

"Where do we fill them?" gasped Ruby.

Dora cried, "Water butt! And there's the horse trough against the wall! Oh, do be quick!"

The maid, Eileen, came running into the yard, followed by a woman who must be the cook. Alex was rather disappointed by the cook. Cooks

in books and on telly were usually middle-aged and round and red-faced and cheerful – this one was about thirty, and was thin and wiry and energetic-looking. Cook behaved in a most un-cookish manner, by running for a fire broom and beating at the flames. Eileen and Hodges took another, and Mary thrust her hose at Ruby and grabbed a third. Dora threw a bucket at Alex and ran towards a stone trough against the wall of the barn. Alex followed. It was half full of cleanish-looking water. He filled the bucket, ran back to the fire, and threw the water on to the flames. It didn't seem to make much difference.

For the next twenty minutes or so, everything was a blur. Run to the water. Fill the bucket. Run

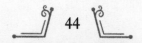

back to the fire. Throw. Run. When the trough was empty, they ran to the water butt instead; this was a large metal barrel filled with rainwater.

For the most part, it all absorbed Alex entirely, but fortunately Mary seemed able to work and think. When Atherton began to flag at the pump, she yelled to Cook to take his place. When Alex felt like he couldn't run any more, she shouted at him to take the hose from Ruby and let her run. Holding the hose wasn't much easier than running, however; it was very hot this close to the fire, and very smoky and hard to breathe. Alex, remembering something he'd read in a book once, turned the hose on to his T-shirt and pulled it up and over his mouth and nose. It helped, a little, but his eyes still stung and were sore with the heat, and he was grateful when Mary yelled, "Dora! Take a turn with the hose!"

It felt like forever before other people began to arrive, pounding up the road from the church. There were perhaps ten or twelve men and women and a couple of children, mostly Pilgrims, he supposed – what a strange thought! Some of them had brought buckets and brooms from the hall, some hadn't, but it didn't matter, because now Mary was yelling at them to form a bucket chain from the water butt, and Atherton – who had taken over the pump again – was relieved of duty, sooty, sweaty and exhausted. But the fire was already out. By the time the fire engine – a rather wonderful-looking old-fashioned red vehicle with the firemen all standing and holding on to the sides – arrived, there was very little for them to do except inspect the damage, smoke cigarettes, and devour the tea and shortbread that Eileen and Cook brought down on tea trays. It tasted just like twenty-first-century tea and shortbread, only the tea was rather strong, and the shortbread slightly sooty.

Dora and Henry and Alex and Ruby sat on the edge of the horse trough and drank their tea and watched. Nearly everyone – well, all of the men, and one or two of the younger women, who Alex supposed must be lady anthropologist friends of Mary's – was smoking. Most of them had cigarettes, but a couple had pipes, and Atherton had a wonderful mother-of-pearl affair with a shiny teak handle.

"Everyone smokes!" said Alex.

"Don't they in the future?" said Dora.

"Well – *some* people do," said Ruby disapprovingly. "But only idiots. Don't you know smoking kills you?"

"I don't think it does," said Dora kindly. "Simply everyone does it, you know, and they're not dead, are they?" She made a sweeping gesture with her arm. Everyone did, indeed, seem not to be dead.

"It does in the end though," Alex said.

Dora didn't seem too worried by this

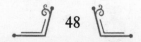

pronouncement. She was more interested in pointing out everyone important who had come up from the hall.

"That's Uncle Edmund. He lives in London and does something frightfully clever for the government. That's Mother – and that's Father there, with the green hat. Uncle Edmund's the oldest brother and Uncle Atherton's the youngest. Father comes in between. Applecott House belongs to Uncle Edmund, but he always says he hates the country, so we live here instead."

"I thought your Uncle Atherton lived here?" said Ruby.

Dora shook her head.

"Uncle Atherton doesn't live anywhere really.

He's always charging about somewhere foreign – before Peru it was Rhodesia, and before Rhodesia it was China, I think, or maybe Japan. Somewhere hot. He just stays here when he comes home, and stores all his antiquities in the hayloft. Mother thought he might settle down when he got married, but it doesn't look like it. He and Miss Flynn are going to Egypt next."

"What do you think was in that box?" said Alex. He hadn't forgotten the packing crate, with its mysterious contents.

Dora shrugged.

"The Newberry Cup?" she said. "It's no earthly good trying to guess what Uncle Atherton brings home. Could be simply anything. It must be a pretty decent antiquity, though, if he and Miss Flynn are so excited about it. Shall we go and see?" And she hopped off the horse trough and ran over to Atherton, who was standing with Mary and Uncle Edmund – a large, red-faced man with a walrus moustache – talking to one of the firemen.

"Started *deliberately*?" Atherton was saying. "My hat! You can't be serious!"

"Uncle Atherton." Henry tugged on his uncle's sleeve. "Can't we see your Cup thing?"

"Cup thing?" Uncle Edmund turned, rather grumpily, to Atherton. "You haven't been bringing *more* junk into the house, have you, Atherton?"

"Eh? What? Oh, no, not at all." Atherton put

a hand on Henry's shoulder and said hurriedly, "Why don't we go back and get you cleaned up, eh? Mary! Are you coming?"

Mary came hurrying over from a huddled conversation with another fireman.

"Atherton, did you hear what they're saying?" she said. "Someone started the fire *deliberately*! I can't believe it! Can you?"

"I don't know," said Atherton. "I did wonder… It isn't as though it's been frightfully hot, and Hodges is very good about not smoking in the stables, although you can't ever be sure, of course."

They made their way slowly up the garden path.

Dora said, "But who would set fire to the stables? And why? What would be the point?"

"I don't know..." said Atherton again, rather thoughtfully. "You haven't got any mortal enemies you've forgotten to tell me about, have you, my angel?"

"Not unless you count that chieftain in Peru," said Mary cheerfully. "And even he rather liked me by the end, I think. And besides, cooking me in boiling oil was more *his* style, not wilful damage to property. Edmund hasn't offended anyone, has he?"

"Half the village, I should have thought," said Atherton. "But I can't *quite* see the good people of Dalton resorting to arson either. I wonder..."

They'd reached the house. Now that they weren't frantically running towards the fire, Alex noticed more differences between Applecott House *then* and Applecott House *now*. Different curtains. Different *windows*. Roses where the modern house was clear. And everything looked *newer* somehow, less tumbledown and shabby. It was disorientating, like seeing a photograph of someone when they were twenty years younger.

The front door was swinging open. Atherton frowned at it and quickened his pace.

"What is it?" said Mary. "Darling?"

"I'm not sure," Atherton said. "Maybe nothing. But all the same..."

He hurried into the hallway and through into the living room. The children followed. His anxiety was catching; Alex could feel himself beginning to worry, although he wasn't sure about what exactly.

The living room was just as they'd left it. The packing cases were still piled up on every piece of available floor. The newest packing case still sat in the middle of the room, the lid lying on the coffee table next to a rather ugly statue of a rearing horse. And Atherton was standing next to the packing case, staring inside.

"Dearest," said Mary, catching something in his frozen expression. "Dearest—"

The children hurried forward and peered into the box.

It was empty.

The Newberry Cup was gone.

CHAPTER FOUR
PLUM CAKE, PINAFORES AND PIRATES

"Things are always happening in 1912, aren't they?" said Alex.

They were in the bathroom upstairs, where they'd been sent to "clean up". Rather to Alex's surprise, bathrooms in 1912 looked fairly similar

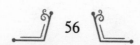

to modern bathrooms, except that the bathtub had brass feet like a lion, there wasn't a shower, and you flushed the toilet by pulling on a chain, which released the water from a cistern above your head.

"Mostly I think things just always happen to Uncle Atherton and Miss Flynn," said Dora, scrubbing at her face with a flannel, and succeeding only in transferring most of the soot back from the flannel and on to her face again. "They nearly got attacked by pirates on their way home from Peru. And besides, this isn't two things, it's one thing really. Whatever rotten beast set that fire obviously did it to get us out of the way, so they could steal that Cup. Oh, bother this soot! I don't see the point of washing when we've all got to have baths tonight anyway."

"We're a *bit* cleaner," said Ruby, studying herself critically in the bathroom mirror.

"Yes," said Dora. "But look here. You simply can't go around in 1912 dressed like that. People will think you've run away from a circus. You might borrow some of our clothes, just until we figure out how to send you back."

"Um," said Alex. He looked at Henry, who had made no attempt to wash himself, but was busy pulling hideous faces at himself in the mirror. "It's all right for you and Ruby. But I'll never fit into Henry's stuff."

"You can borrow some of Dickie's things,"

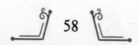

said Dora. "He's our cousin," she explained. "On Mother's side. Our aunt is always sending us his hand-me-downs for Henry to grow into. Come on. I'll show you."

Dora's and Henry's bedrooms were nothing like Ruby's and Alex's. Henry slept in what was apparently called the "night nursery", a room with two beds – one for Henry and one for the nursery maid, who had left last year. The walls were still papered with characters from nursery rhymes, something Henry was rather scornful about. There was a "day nursery" attached, with a rocking horse – a different rocking horse to the one in Aunt Joanna's playroom, a much more exciting-looking rocking horse on its own rockers, unlike Aunt Joanna's, which hung from a sort of trestle – a bookcase full of hardbacked books, and a battered cupboard full of toys. Alex had a look at the bookcase. There were some books he recognised: *Just So Stories* and *Peter Rabbit* and *Alice Through the Looking-Glass*. But most he had never heard of: *Stalky and Co.*, *The Story of a Short Life*, *Mother Goose*...

Dora had her own bedroom, which was very neat; it reminded Alex rather of the guests' rooms in Aunt Joanna's house, although the bed-and-breakfast guests didn't have iron bedsteads, or eiderdowns and counterpanes, or a dressing table with a silver-backed hairbrush and a washstand with a heavy china basin and jug with shepherdesses on it. Unlike Ruby's bedroom at home, which was covered in posters of rock bands and photographs of Ruby and her friends, and screamed *"nearly a teenager!"*, Dora's room looked rather grown up. Only the pictures of ladies in ballgowns, cut out of magazines and stuck up around the mirror, the books in the bookcase, and the three rag dolls lolling rather sadly on the window sill suggested that this room belonged to a child at all.

Clothes in 1912 were weird. Boys and girls apparently wore long underwear – like a sort of vest-and-pants-all-in-one combination. Ruby refused to even try them on.

"Aren't you *boiling*?" she said. "It's summer!"

But for girls, she soon discovered, things quickly got even worse. Over the combinations, Ruby was expected to wear petticoats, something called a liberty bodice, which was somewhere between a corset and a vest, and black stockings. On top of *that*, a 1912 girl wore a long dress, a white pinafore and – if she was going outside – a hat.

"This is *ridiculous*!" Ruby said furiously. "In *our* time you wear sundresses in summer! Bare legs! Sandals!"

"Well," said Alex, trying to be fair. "In our time, we've got climate change." But even he had to admit that Dora and Ruby looked rather hot in all their layers.

"That does sound nice," Dora said rather wistfully, looking at Ruby's blue jeans and fitted T-shirt. "But isn't it frightfully indecent?"

"Someone," said Ruby grimly, "should teach you lot about feminism."

Clothes for boys were better. Without the combinations, Henry's cousin's grey knickerbockers and jacket, shirt and straw hat seemed almost reasonable (though the shirt did come with a detachable Eton collar, which was *very* weird). Alex was feeling rather smug, until he saw the last item Henry was pulling out.

"Stockings! Black stockings!"

Dora and Henry looked at him blankly.

"No!" said Alex firmly. "No way. Boys do not

wear stockings. Not in the future. Not ever!"

But it appeared that in 1912, they did. The only socks Henry owned were a pair of white ankle socks bought for dancing class, and far too small for Alex, even if he could have brought himself to wear them. Ruby was unsympathetic.

"At least you can run!" she said.

Downstairs, someone was banging a gong.

"Tea!" said Dora. "Are you hungry? I'm simply ravenous."

On their way back down, Alex stopped by the mirror. It stood, looking just as it always had in Aunt Joanna's hallway, innocently reflecting the green-and-yellow wallpaper and the white front

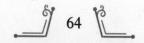

door. He touched it. Nothing happened.

"Do you think we're stuck here forever?"

It was Ruby. Alex didn't know how to answer.

"I hope not," he said, rather inadequately.

"I've been thinking," she said. "About that wish you made. Do you think it had something to do with that? Like, I bet that Cup is worth thousands and thousands of pounds, don't you? So perhaps it got stolen, and that's why Aunt Joanna's poor now. Well, poor-ish." No one who owned Applecott House could possibly be described as poor. "So maybe there was a genie in that bottle, and it's granting your wish. If we can find the Cup, then Atherton wouldn't have lost it, and then he'll have all that money, and then Aunt Joanna can inherit it, and everyone will be happy, and we can go home."

"Maybe," said Alex doubtfully. That morning he would have said he didn't believe in magic *or* wishes. But a lot had happened since that morning. "Wouldn't a genie just put the money in Aunt Joanna's bank account though? That's what I'd do."

"It wasn't a genie though, was it?" said Ruby. "It was a pile of dust. Maybe it didn't have enough magic left."

"Or maybe," said Alex, "it's nothing to do with that bottle. Maybe it's just a time-travelling mirror. We should ask Atherton where he got it from, and if he knows how to work it."

"He doesn't know it can send you through time," said Ruby. Alex had to agree. Atherton hadn't looked at all like he believed in time travel when Henry had brought it up that morning. "In books," she went on, "kids always have to fix something before they can solve whatever their problem is. Like, if there's a ghost, you have to sort out the ghost's problem, and then it stops haunting the house. Or you have to not kill your grandfather or whatever. So maybe it's got nothing to do with your stupid genie. Maybe there's a problem here that needs fixing, and when we fix it we can go home."

"That's the Cup again," said Alex.

"Yes…" said Ruby thoughtfully. She pressed

her finger against the glass. Then she laughed. "Come on," she said. "Let's get some tea. We can worry about that stupid Cup later."

Neither Alex nor Ruby had a very clear idea of what tea would involve. Alex was picturing the sort of high tea farmers' wives always served in Famous Five novels, with whole roast ham, and homemade bread, and apple pie. Ruby was hoping for afternoon tea, the sort with china cups you drank your tea out of with your little finger sticking out, and cakes on silver cake stands, and cucumber sandwiches with the crusts cut off.

What was actually brought into the room (which in Aunt Joanna's house was the room set aside for bed-and-breakfast guests to sit in, but here was apparently the drawing room) was a solid-looking teapot, a plate of bread and butter, a jar of strawberry jam, and something the children had never seen before, but Dora said was plum cake.

"Don't you have plum cake in the future?" said Henry in astonishment.

"I don't think so," said Alex. "We have lots of other things though," he added hastily. "Chocolate fingers, and Mini Rolls, and carrot cake—"

"*Carrot* cake!" said Henry, and nearly fell off his seat, he was laughing so hard.

"It's nicer than it sounds," said Alex, but Dora and Henry looked horrified.

They were halfway through their second slices of cake when Atherton and Mary appeared, both looking much cleaner than the children had managed (although Atherton did have a suspicious-looking black tidemark behind the ears).

"What ho!" said Atherton. "Oh, cake! Three loud cheers!"

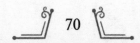

And he ignored the bread and butter and went straight for the cake knife, cutting himself an enormous slice, which he devoured with great enthusiasm.

"Someone's taken something down to the wedding guests, haven't they?" said Mary, watching him with amusement as she poured the tea.

"I told Eileen to see to it, oh my best beloved," said Atherton. "They seemed to have mostly avoided total sootification and decided to get back to decking the halls. Edmund said we were to join them once we'd cleaned up. I suppose you kids had better come too," he added doubtfully, looking at Alex and Ruby. "*Who* did you say you were, exactly?"

"I *told* you!" said Henry indignantly. "They came from the future!"

"Oh, Henry, do chuck it," said Atherton. It was hard to think of him as a grown-up; he behaved much more like an overgrown teenager.

"We do though," said Alex. "Ruby, show him your phone."

Ruby felt in her bag. Then she had another rummage. Then she tipped the bag upside down, so house keys, purse, hairbrush and an odd collection of receipts, fluff and sweet wrappers fell on to the floor.

"It's gone!"

"What do you mean, it's gone?" said Alex.

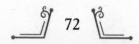

"My phone! It's not there! Someone's stolen it!"

"Maybe it just fell out," said Dora, helpfully.

"It did not!" said Ruby, furiously. "Someone's *stolen* it! And I know who, too! It was that boy! The one who brought in those crates with Hodges. He bumped against me when he came in! *And* he grabbed me! I thought he was trying to pinch my bum or something, but he wasn't! He was stealing my phone!"

"Why would he steal your phone?" said Alex, practically. "He wouldn't even know what it was."

"I'm afraid your friend's probably right," said Atherton. "That's Frank, the gardener's boy. He *does* steal things, little wretch. Go down and ask for it back – he won't mind. He's used to it."

"Uncle Atherton's right," said Dora. "I'm frightfully sorry, but nobody's ever been able to stop him. He doesn't mean anything by it."

"He doesn't mean anything by *stealing*?" said Ruby. She looked at Alex, who shrugged.

"He doesn't though," said Dora. "He's ... a bit simple. He just likes collecting things."

She stood up.

"Come on. I expect he's down at the stables with Hodges, helping clear up. Let's go and find him."

"And *then* you'll see!" said Henry to Atherton.

"Top hole," said Atherton. He leaned over and cut himself another slice of cake.

CHAPTER FIVE
FLAT CAPS, BOWLER HATS AND BOATERS

The stables were looking rather sorry for themselves in the late afternoon sunshine. The firemen and all the wedding guests had gone, and all that was left of the disaster was the blackened stone walls and burned beams of the stables. Up close, Alex could see that the damage wasn't too bad; the door and interior woodwork – and of course the straw – were completely burned away, but the walls were solid stone, and the roof was tile, and these were soot-blackened but intact.

Hodges was busy dousing the burned wood with buckets of water, presumably to make sure that the fire was completely out. Dora and Henry ran over to him.

"Darling Hodges! Is it all completely ruined?"

"Is the stable going to fall down?"

Alex had thought servants were people you bossed around, but Dora and Henry seemed to consider them an extension of the family. Hodges seemed to agree. He put down the bucket and beamed at them fondly.

"Nay," he said. "We'll put it right. It's just the woodwork that's gone. Mr Pilgrim said he'd get an architect chappie he knows to come down and have a look at it. I told him we can put up stalls without an architect, but Mr Pilgrim, he said the beams and whatnot need to be right."

"Did you hear?" said Henry. "Someone lit the fire, then stole Uncle Atherton's new antiquity!"

"It's true," said Dora. "Isn't that perfectly beastly? Wherever are the horses going to sleep?"

"Don't you fret about the horses, Miss Dora," said Hodges. "Mrs Pinkerton said she'd take them until the stables were fixed up. You'll be able to go over and ride whenever you want."

"Good-o!" said Henry.

"Mrs Pinkerton's a brick," Dora agreed. "Hodges, do you know where Frank is?"

"Nay," said Hodges. "Not since we brought those crates in for your uncle. But you know what Frank's like. He's probably up to some mischief. If you see him, you tell him from me, there's plenty of work needs doing here and he's not paid to lollygag."

Hodges, Dora explained, was the gardener, groom and odd-job man. Frank was his son and was paid a small wage to help his father with the extra garden work in the summer holidays.

He was discovered without much effort behind one of the potting sheds, bent over some objects in a heap on the floor. He started rather guiltily when he saw Dora.

"Frank!" she said. "Whatever are you doing here? Have you been taking things again?"

Frank grinned a little sheepishly but didn't answer.

Dora held out her hand.

"Come on," she said. "Hand 'em over. You know you can't take things without asking."

Frank dug his hand in his pocket and brought out a rather curious handful of small objects: Ruby's phone, a china shepherdess, and the bag of sweets Henry and Dora had been fighting over in the mirror. Dora took them gravely.

"That was very wrong of you, Frank," she said,

and he gave her another sheepish grin and ducked his head.

"Here," she said, handing the phone to Ruby and the paper bag to Henry, but Ruby was busy looking at the heap of things Frank had been evidently in the middle of trying to conceal.

"What's that?" she demanded.

Frank looked panicked. "Nothing!" he said. "It's nothing!"

"It is *not* nothing," said Ruby. She darted forward, and the others followed. Now Alex could see what Frank had been hiding. A can of petrol. A box of matches. Some rags.

"You started the fire!" he cried. "Did you steal the Cup too?"

Frank was shaking his head.

"Not me, not me," he said. "They told me to!"

"Who told you to?" said Dora. Frank shook his head again.

"Frank, this is serious," said Dora. "Those brutes who told you to set the fire – they've stolen something important from Uncle Atherton. You have to tell us who they were, so we can find it. Were they someone you knew?"

Frank was shaking his head. "Just men," he said. "Men at the station."

"You don't know their names?" said Alex hopefully.

Frank shook his head. There was a despondent pause. Then he said brightly, "They're staying in Mrs Pinkerton's coach house. Come down last night, they did."

"Oh!" said Dora. "Oh, Frank, thank you!"

Frank beamed.

"Let's go and find them!" said Ruby.

"We should tell Uncle Atherton and Miss Flynn," said Dora.

"No time," said Alex. "They've probably left already. I would, wouldn't you? Someone needs to go and get help, and someone needs to go and stop them leaving, if they're still there."

Dora bit her lip.

"Henry," she said. "You run and get Uncle Atherton. He'll know what to do. We'll go to the coach house. And hurry!"

Mrs Pinkerton lived on the other side of the village. In Alex and Ruby's time, her house was a Hotel and Spa with Extensive Grounds. Alex and Ruby's parents had taken them there for lunch once, to celebrate some relation's birthday, and there had been grown-ups wandering around in dressing gowns, and fancy lemonade in glass bottles, and three different types of bread in a basket. It was funny to think that in 1912, just one family lived in it.

A coach house turned out to be exactly what it sounded like: a building designed to keep coaches in, sort of like a 1912 garage. There was a coach in there now, and an old-fashioned-looking car, and another car parked in the driveway. At the side of the coach house was a set of stone steps leading up to the second storey, where there were evidently some sort of living quarters. A man in a black suit and a bowler hat was coming down the steps, a suitcase in each hand, evidently about to load them into the car. He glanced up at the children, but didn't speak.

"Do you think that's one of Frank's men?" Alex whispered to Dora. Dora shrugged. The man looked rather like a servant, a butler perhaps. It occurred to him that stopping someone driving a car out of a building designed to store cars in was perhaps not the best way of catching a criminal. What if they tried to arrest Mrs Pinkerton's

chauffeur by mistake? On the other hand, he *had* come from the rooms above the coach house. Presumably those suitcases belonged to *someone*, and presumably that someone would come to claim them.

He did. A moment later, a second man appeared, a young man about Atherton's age, with red hair and freckles. Even Alex could see that this man was better dressed than the man who looked like a butler; he was wearing a flannel suit rather like Atherton's and a flat straw boater rather like a grown-up version of the hat Alex was wearing. Neither of the men looked like storybook robbers. They looked like a young gentleman and his servant.

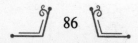

"Look!" hissed Ruby, and pointed.

For a moment, Alex couldn't understand what she meant. Then he saw it. A piece of straw, attached to the young man's sleeve. A piece of straw looking suspiciously similar to the straw in which the Newberry Cup had been packed.

"It's them!" Ruby said excitedly. The man who looked like a butler put the suitcases in the back of the car, shut the door and climbed into the passenger seat. "And they're about to get away! We have to delay them!"

"*How?*" said Alex, but Ruby was already hurrying forward.

"Hello!" she said brightly. "We're ... er ... collecting for ... er..."

She shot a meaningful look at Dora, who said, "The Missionary Aid Society" at once.

"Yeah!" said Ruby. "Them. We want to aid missionaries. Would you care to make a donation? It's very good work, um, converting heathens and so forth."

"Not right now, kiddies," said the man in the straw hat. "We're in a hurry."

"Oh, but it won't take long," said Ruby earnestly. She moved between the man and the car door. "Let me tell you about all the good work they're doing in … Africa. And Asia! And Australia! Probably! Singing hymns! Exploring jungles!"

Alex was pretty sure missionaries didn't explore jungles. The young man didn't seem to think so

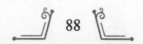

either.

"All right," he said. "Very nice. Move along now." And he made a shooing gesture at Ruby. Ruby didn't move.

"And another thing!" she said. "Before you go! Have you seen my dog? I've lost him. He's about this big – he's white – his name is Samuel, but he answers to Sammy. He's—"

"No, I have not!" said the young man. "Look here. I'm in a frightful hurry. I don't know what sort of game you're playing at, but if you'd kindly move aside, I'll be getting along."

Dora cast an agonised look at Alex.

"But you can't!" she said, before Alex could stop her.

The man who looked like a butler opened the passenger door and got out of the car. The other man's face still looked vaguely irritated, but the butler's face had a sudden air of menace, which alarmed Alex. For the first time since they'd arrived, he was afraid.

"And why not?" said the butler.

"Um," said Alex. "No reason. Of course you can go. The girls are just being silly – we're playing a game. Come on, Ruby, let's leave them alone."

The man in the straw hat looked relieved.

"That's right," he said. "Very funny. Let me get in my car, will you?"

"But we can't!" said Dora. She stamped her foot. "We can't let them go! They've got Uncle

Atherton's Cup!"

There was an awful silence. Ruby and Alex glared at Dora. The man in the straw hat glanced at the man who looked like a butler, who shut the car door with a meaningful *clunk* and moved, slowly and deliberately, round to stand behind the children.

"*What* did you just say?" he said.

"Nothing!" said Alex. He grabbed Dora's wrist. "She said you've got her uncle up! Yes! Up – er – upset! He gets very upset with people who don't give to charity, doesn't he, Dora? Why don't we go away now and ask some other people for donations, rather than waste time with these people? I'm sure they've got other things they ought to be doing."

Ruby gave him an uncertain look.

The man in the straw hat said, "Giles!"

The man who looked like a butler and was probably Giles said, "Yes, sir," meaningfully. He put his hand on Ruby's shoulder. "What's your game then?" he said. "Trying to delay us, are you? You haven't called the police, have you, or anything like that?"

"Yes, we have!" said Dora. "And we've told them exactly where you're staying, and who you are, and that we were coming to stop you! So if you try and do anything to us, they'll know it was you, and they'll come after you!"

The younger man glanced at Giles, who shook his head.

"I doubt it, sir," he said. "Can't see the police letting some kids come after a pair of dangerous criminals on their own. I expect she sent someone to find her uncle, that's all."

He put his hand in his trouser pocket and pulled out a piece of wood, wrapped in leather, about thirty centimetres long. He held it in one hand and began to tap it, slowly and threateningly against the other. It was, very clearly, a weapon.

"Would you like me to take care of it, sir?" he said.

CHAPTER SIX
"VENOMOUS SNAKES ARE NOTHING ON THIS."

Alex had read quite a lot of books with fights in them. He'd even been to judo class – once – with his friend Oliver, but he'd found it hard to take it seriously. The white pyjamas everyone had to wear had just made him want to giggle.

He was rather ashamed, therefore, of how quickly the fight with the two men was over. Giles had simply put his arms around Ruby, lifted her up, and carried her kicking and yelling into the coach house, where he shut the door and pulled the bolt across. Alex had run after him to unbolt the door, and the same thing had happened to him; he'd been lifted up and unceremoniously dumped inside beside Ruby. For a butler, Giles was pretty strong.

Dora, meanwhile, had bolted in the direction of the big house, yelling at the top of her voice, "Help! Help! We're being *kidnapped*!"

Unfortunately, to get to the big house you had to go through a gate, which was locked, and while Dora was climbing over it, the man in the straw hat had managed to grab her and drag her backwards. Dora continued yelling, but this gave her rather less breath to fight with, and it wasn't difficult even for the man in the straw hat – who wasn't particularly athletic-looking – to overpower her. Ruby had nearly managed to escape when he opened the door to push Dora in, but both men were now outside, and they forced the door shut easily enough. Then the children heard a bolt being drawn across. Then what sounded like a padlock being attached. Then they heard voices – though not what was said – decreasing in volume as the men moved away. Then the sound of doors slamming, a sputter as an engine started and the sound of the car driving away.

And then there was nothing.

Dora spoke first.

"Is everyone all right?" she said. "Those pigs didn't hurt you, did they?"

"No," said Ruby grimly. "I might have hurt *them* though." Alex could hear both of them fumbling in the dark. Then, at the same time, Dora lit a match and Ruby found the torch on her phone, and suddenly they could see.

"An electric torch!" said Dora, sounding impressed.

At the same time Ruby said, "You carry *matches* in your pocket? You really are something out of

Swallows and Amazons, aren't you?"

"What?" said Dora.

Ruby said, "I meant out of an old-fashioned kids' book. Kids in books always carry knives and handkerchiefs and bullseyes and stuff around with them. I never understood why."

Dora looked baffled.

"Bullseyes are sweets," she said, like Ruby was an idiot. "And you blow your nose on your handkerchief. Don't you have handkerchiefs in the future?"

"No," said Ruby. "We have tissues. How often do you *actually* use matches though? I mean, seriously?"

"How often do you use your torch?" said Dora,

defensively. Ruby opened her mouth to explain about mobile phones, and also the *ridiculous* bedtimes her parents thought were sensible to impose on someone who was nearly a teenager.

Alex, who had been exploring the coach house, interrupted. "There's a window," he said. "But I don't think any of us could fit through it, even if we could break it. There's an axe. Maybe we could break down the door?"

Ruby and Dora stopped arguing and looked doubtfully at the coach-house door, which was big and solid and probably very expensive and bothersome to replace even if they *did* manage to hack it down. Then they looked at Alex's axe, which looked more the sort of thing designed to chop logs into kindling than to actually chop down trees.

"I don't think we can *break down the door*," said Dora. "Mrs Pinkerton would be jolly upset with us."

"She'd be even more upset if she found our mouldering corpses in here," said Ruby, crossly.

"We wouldn't actually *moulder*," said Alex. "Henry knows where we are. He'll find us eventually."

"Oh," said Ruby. "*Eventually*. Great. When those men will be *miles* away. In *Sweden*, probably, spending their ill-gotten gains on ... I dunno ... saunas and stuff. While we're stuck here." She eyed Mrs Pinkerton's car, which was parked in the middle of the coach-house floor. "How difficult are 1912 cars to drive, do you think? I bet we could break down that door if we drove a car into it."

"We *couldn't*," said Dora looking shocked. "Motor cars are frightfully dear. We can't drive one into a *door*."

"They aren't as expensive as that Cup, I bet," said Ruby mutinously, but since neither she nor Alex knew how to drive, the point was somewhat moot.

"Maybe there are other people around," Dora suggested. "We could shout?" Ruby looked rather put out that someone besides herself had come up with a good idea, and, after some argument about what to shout, they counted to three and all yelled, "HELP!"

Then, because it was rather good fun, they did it again.

"HELP! HELP!"

"WE'RE IN THE COACH HOUSE!" Alex added, but it didn't do any good. No one came.

Ruby and Dora sat on a pile of logs. Ruby said she was trying to conserve her energy, which would

be useful if they really did start to starve to death. Alex thought this was ridiculous but he didn't say so. He took Ruby's phone and carried on exploring the coach house, in case someone had helpfully left a key lying about or something. But no one had. In the end, he came and sat with the girls, and tried not to give in to despair.

"What *is* the future like?" said Dora. "You never told us."

Neither Ruby nor Alex were quite sure how to answer this.

"Well," said Alex. "There's computers. And mobile phones, and televisions, and – and vacuum cleaners, and electricity—"

"We've got electricity!" said Dora. "We've got

our own generator."

"Everyone has electricity in the future," said Ruby. "Well, everyone in Britain. And most people have cars. And no one has servants – not unless you're really, really posh – like the Queen, or something. Not live-in servants, anyway. Like, my friend Charlotte has a cleaner, but no one has cooks and parlourmaids and butlers."

"Do you have machines that cook for you?" said Dora interestedly.

"Well," said Alex, "we've got microwaves."

"And no one wears stupid bodices and petticoats and combinations," said Ruby, warming to her subject. "Girls just wear sensible clothes like jeans and trainers. *And* we can vote."

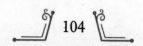

"Honest Injun?" Dora looked delighted.

Ruby said, "We don't call people Injuns in the future either. *Or* Red Indians. It's racist."

"It's *what*?"

"It's a bad word," Ruby explained. "You should say Native American instead."

Dora looked puzzled. "Well, anyway," she said. "What's going to happen next in history? Are people from Mars going to land or something?"

Alex hesitated. 1912. Both he and Ruby knew what came next in history. Alex wasn't sure it was a good idea to tell people about the horrible things in their immediate future, but Ruby didn't seem to care.

"The First World War is next," she announced.

"It's a big war, with the Germans and—" She stopped. Everyone called it the First *World* War, but in school people mostly just talked about Germany and England. "And the French," she said hesitantly. "And – and – the Americans. I think. And lots of other people too," she added hastily. "And everyone goes off and fights in trenches, and their feet fall off cos of trench foot, and there are rats and tanks and things. And war horses."

"Ruby!" Alex said. "You can't tell people something like that's going to happen to them!"

But Dora didn't seem that upset.

"*Tanks?*" she said. "Tanks of what?"

"Um..." said Alex, but Dora didn't wait for an answer.

"People don't fight wars in trenches," she went on. Her talking-to-idiots voice was back. "Except moats, maybe. They fight on battlefields. Or they besiege people."

"Not in this war they didn't," said Alex. "I mean, they're going to not. They live in trenches. And then they climb over the top and get shot."

"Well, that's stupid," said Dora. "They should have just had a big battle and then the winner should be whoever's left at the end. Why don't they do that?"

Ruby and Alex glanced at each other. They'd both studied the First World War in school. But nobody had been very clear on why the soldiers didn't just have a big battle and decide who'd won based on who was left at the end.

"*And,*" Dora went on triumphantly, "you can't keep horses in trenches. You keep horses in fields. I think you must have got muddled," she went on, kindly. "History *is* awfully muddling sometimes. All those kings and barons and Roman emperors and whatnot."

"Me?" said Ruby indignantly. "*Muddled?*"

But Alex held up a hand. "Shut up!" he said.

Ruby glared. "I don't see why *I*—" she began.

"There's someone there!" said Alex. "Can't you hear them?"

They all listened as hard as they could. Alex was *sure* he could hear someone. Footsteps, crunching down the path. Voices.

"Help!" he yelled. The others yelled too.

"Help! We're in here! Help!"

The footsteps crunched closer to the coach house.

"Hullo! Is that you, kids?"

Every heart in the coach house simultaneously leapt. Every heart knew that voice.

"Yes!" Dora called. "Yes, it's us! Those beasts locked us in!"

"Just a tick." Atherton sounded cheerful. "Hang on – I say, this lock's frightfully stiff, isn't it? Ah!"

The door pulled back. Light streamed into the coach house. There, standing in the doorway, were Atherton and Mary, with Henry bobbing excitedly between them.

"Golly!" said Henry.

"Another crisis!" said Mary cheerfully. "You lot are almost making me nostalgic for Peru. Venomous snakes are nothing on this."

CHAPTER SEVEN
ADVENTURES AT HIGH SPEED

"We came as quickly as ever we could," Henry was explaining. "Uncle Atherton has the most ripping motor car – it goes ever so fast!"

"Jolly considerate robbers you've got here," Atherton was saying. "Leaving the key in the lock

like that. Somehow I don't think we're dealing with hardened criminals, do you, my love?"

They were tramping through the grass to the road. Ruby and Dora had explained all about the Cup and the men and the dreadful fact of their escape. Atherton and Mary seemed far less astonished by all this than Alex had expected.

"What did they look like?" Atherton asked. "Can you remember?"

"Um..." Ruby hesitated. "Brown hair? Youngish?"

"There were two of them," said Alex. "One was posh—"

"Posh?"

"He talked like you. You know, all la-di-da. The

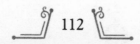

other one looked like a butler."

"He wasn't a *butler*," said Dora. "He was a valet." Ruby and Alex looked at her blankly. "You know. Like a maid, but if you're a man. They press your suits and clean your shoes and do your housework. Father used to have one, before we moved here."

"You mean like Jeeves?" said Ruby.

"Who?"

"*Anyway*," said Alex. "The servant was called Giles. And the posh one had a grey suit and a straw hat and a green car with one of those roofs that go down when it's sunny. And he didn't have brown hair – he was ginger. He was about your age. Giles was older."

"Huh," said Atherton. "I rather think you kids

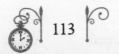

had better come with me."

They'd come out of the garden and on to the road, where another old-fashioned car was parked. This one was much fancier than the green car, however. It was bigger, for one thing, and lower, and shinier, and sort of sleeker. It looked rather as if, had it been made a hundred years later, it would have been a sports car.

"That's Uncle Atherton's motor car," Henry said. "It's A1! It goes ever so fast. I bet it goes faster than whatever car those rotten burglars had."

"But," said Ruby, "how can you chase them? You don't know which way they went!"

Mary looked at her somewhat in surprise.

"We'll ask," she said. "It's not like people won't

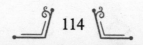

have noticed a motor car. They make a frightful racket."

"And," said Atherton, "I rather think I know where they were going." As he spoke, he was putting on a new layer of very interesting-looking clothes: leather gloves; a long, thin, brown coat; and a pair of goggles that made him look like Mr Toad. "Hop in, would you, my angel? Dora, your mother was asking what I'd done with you. Can you and Henry nip back and tell her I haven't sold you into slavery?"

Atherton lifted the car's bonnet and began fiddling with the engine. Alex couldn't see exactly what he was doing, but it looked a lot more complicated than turning an ignition key. "And

115

on the way," he continued, "could you pop into the police station and tell Inspector Heggarty that I think I know who took the Newberry Cup and we're in hot pursuit, and if he wanted to follow, I'd be much obliged? Tell him we're taking the London road. You two –" this was directed at Alex and Ruby – "I'm still not entirely sure who you are, but if you haven't got to step through a looking glass in the next half an hour, could you jump in the bus and point out these men to us if we spot them?"

"Bus?" said Alex.

"He means the motor car," said Henry. "Oh, lucky, lucky you! You have to go ever so fast when you're chasing a robber, don't you, Uncle

Atherton?"

"You do," said Atherton. "And you kids might help a fellow catch a robber by *getting in the damn motor car.*"

He threw something at Alex, who caught it. It was a pair of Mr Toad goggles. Alex and Ruby looked at each other and scrambled into the back seat. Atherton, meanwhile, had inserted a handle in the front of the car and was winding it furiously.

The car sputtered to itself, and then started, with a delicious *ku-ku-ku-ku-wrrrrhhhoooum.*

Alex had never been in a vintage car before. He had never even been in an open-topped car before. It was quite different to modern driving.

For one thing, there were no seat belts – not even for Mary and Atherton. For another, even though they weren't actually going that fast, it *felt* faster because you got the wind rushing through your hair, and of course you jolted around the back of the car every time Atherton took a corner a bit too fast, which he did a lot. Alex wondered if driving tests had been invented in 1912. Judging by Atherton's driving, he thought it unlikely.

Then, too, the roads were quite unlike modern

roads. Tarmac had evidently not been invented yet – the car threw up an enormous cloud of dust, which made Alex very grateful for the goggles. Nor, apparently, had anyone figured out that roads that were generally flat and not full of holes might be a good idea. The long car bumped and jumped and rattled over every pothole. Ruby looked rather green, but Atherton showed no signs of slowing down.

Mary gripped her hat with her hand and said,

"Atherton! Darling!"

"What?" said Atherton, taking a corner at such speed that Alex had to duck to avoid an unexpected tree branch. Henry's cousin's straw hat flew off and landed in the grass at the side of the road. Ruby took off Dora's hat and, very definitely, sat on it. "Too fast?"

"Actually, it's rather thrilling," Mary said. Atherton took his eyes off the road long enough to kiss her. Alex shut his eyes tight and gripped the seat with both hands. Ruby squealed.

"You are both *insane!*" she shouted.

Besides the lack of tarmac (and other assorted usefulnesses, like cats' eyes, road markings and speed-limit signs, not to mention pylons), the countryside they were driving through was different in lots of little ways. Instead of neat, regimented fields of potatoes and oilseed rape, the fields were full of wonderfully messy wheat of all different sizes. In amongst the wheat were flowers: poppies and tall daisies, and others that Alex didn't recognise. There were more birds too. And a lot more insects – bees and butterflies in the hedgerows, and the windscreen as they drove was spattered with flies.

And yet, at the same time, it was disorientingly familiar. People looked like people. Trees looked like trees. Grass looked like grass.

"Who do you think this thief is then?" Mary said. "Do you have a whole set of mortal enemies

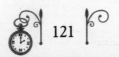

you forgot to tell me about, along with all those relations?"

"No," said Atherton. The car bounced into a pothole and out again, rattling the whole vehicle (along with Alex and Ruby) and – Alex was sure – lifting them both several centimetres into the air and down again. Suspension was also something no one had got around to thinking about in 1912. "Just a chap I know with a habit of leaping before he looks. Which, if you think about it, is dashed obvious. It *must* have been someone who knew we owned those stables. *And* where we'd put those crates. And that I had the Cup, for that matter."

"He could have asked the boy, surely?" said Mary.

"He could," said Atherton. "But the boy didn't know what was in the boxes. Why, even *you* didn't know until I told you."

"I suppose I didn't," said Mary. She looked thoughtful. "Who *did* know?"

"Well," said Atherton. "It rather depends who Charlie Higgins told, doesn't it? But going by that description…"

He swerved to avoid a farmer, who had appeared rather suddenly out of a gate. The farmer leapt back, looking startled. Atherton gave him a cheery wave and honked on the horn.

"Atherton," said Mary accusingly. "I do believe you're enjoying yourself."

"Darling," said Atherton. "I believe you are too.

Did I mention recently how much I love you?"

"Ass," said Mary. She sat back in her seat, looking pleased with herself. "And for God's sake, mind that cow!"

Alex had just about decided that being driven about the countryside by Atherton was only bearable if he kept his eyes *clenched* shut, held on *very* tight to the seat and thought *very hard* about maths, when Ruby yelled, "Stop! That's their car!"

It was. The car was parked in the yard beside a country pub called The White Swan. In Alex's day, pubs had car parks. In 1912, they apparently had stables, with stable yards. Atherton braked rather more dramatically than was strictly necessary, and swerved the car into the stable yard, narrowly avoiding a boy in a flat cap, who gawped at him admiringly.

"You," said Ruby furiously, "are a *terrible* driver."

Atherton tipped his hat to her and scrambled out of the car.

"Come on!" he yelled, and headed towards the pub. Mary and the children followed.

The inside of the pub was divided into little rooms, with horse brasses hanging from the walls. The tables were plain wood, and there were no menus, no pumps serving Coke and Fanta, and no beer pumps with the names of different beers attached to them, although there *were* advertisements behind the bar. *The Doctors' Special Rum, Prescribed by the Medical Profession*, one said. *Finest Ales & Porter, Bottled Ales & Stout*, said another. The pub also smelled rather unpleasantly of cigarette smoke. And – Alex realised, looking around – with the exception of the young woman serving behind the bar, there were no women in it. Were women not allowed to go into pubs?

Atherton strode forwards, the others at his heels. Alex spotted them first. "There they are!" he cried.

There they were, indeed. The younger man and the older, in a corner of the pub, eating what looked like bread and cheese. (Alex and Ruby's parents liked the sort of holidays that involved walking up hills in the middle of nowhere, so the children had eaten in quite a lot of pubs, and they didn't think bread and cheese was at all the sort of food pubs ought to serve. In the twenty-first century it would have been scampi and chips.)

The two men jumped, and the younger one (he'd taken off his straw hat, and his hair looked even redder without it) said, "Great Scott!"

But Atherton cried, "You!"

CHAPTER EIGHT
UPSET

The man with red hair blushed, and his mouth opened and shut without saying anything.

"Charlie!" said Atherton. "What in the devil's name are you doing locking my relations in coach houses? If you're going to do things like that, couldn't you at least pick Auntie Mildred, or that self-important brother of mine, rather than some of the nice ones?"

"Charlie?" whispered Ruby to Alex.

"He was the person Atherton bought the Newberry Cup off," Alex whispered back. "Remember?"

He'd been wondering all the way here if this was the person Atherton had meant when he'd talked about his friend who "leapt before he looked". Who else would know that Atherton had the Cup?

"Atherton!" said Charlie. He got to his feet, knocking the chair over in his hurry, and rubbed his hands nervously on his trousers. "Just a bit of a joke, old man, that's all. No harm done, eh?"

"Well, I wouldn't say that," said Atherton. "Not when my brother's stables are in ruins and my valuable artefact appears to have been stolen. Game's up, Charlie. Why don't you tell me exactly what's going on?"

Charlie had the grace to look uncomfortable.

"Look here, old thing," he said. "Frightfully sorry and all that, but it isn't my artefact, you know. It belongs to Father, and, well … I'd thought it would be simply weeks before he came home and noticed it was gone, by which time I'd be in India. But it turns out he's coming home on Tuesday, and it'll be frightfully awkward, you see. And I *need* that money; I always was a fool about money, and there are all sorts of people who need paying back rather sharpish."

"You could have got a job!" Ruby said indignantly.

Mary grinned.

Alex nudged Ruby and whispered, "I don't think rich people had jobs in the olden days. Not the sort of people who have valets. They always live off allowances and things in books."

"See here," Charlie was saying. "I didn't mean any trouble – honestly, I didn't. How about I just pay you back and we leave it at that? I'm sure you can think of something to put the bobbies off the scent, can't you?"

He gave his friend such an appealing look that Alex was sure Atherton would relent. And

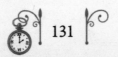

Atherton, indeed, said, rather regretfully, "Well … look here, old thing—"

But they had reckoned without Mary.

"Now, just you wait a minute!" she said. "All of that old-school-tie rot might work with Atherton, but it jolly well won't work with me! He bought that Cup from you fair and square, and if that puts you in a spot with your father, well, that's your affair, isn't it?"

Charlie looked alarmed. He glanced pleadingly at Atherton, who raised both hands as though to say, "Nothing to do with me, mate!" But Mary was still going strong.

"You," she went on, clearly enjoying herself, "are a worm of the highest order! If it were up to me, I'd have you arrested! A couple of years in a nice cold cell and you'll soon change your tune!"

If Charlie had looked panicked before, now he looked terrified. The valet – Giles – on the other hand, wore rather a calculating expression. His eyes darted towards the door. Ruby grabbed Alex's arm.

"Wait there," she said, and slipped away.

"See here…" Charlie was saying. "I didn't … you wouldn't—"

"Oh, wouldn't I just? And I will too! We've called the police, you know. They're on their way, and if you don't hand over our Cup *right now*, we'll hand *you* over to *them*!"

Giles got to his feet with an air of subtle menace.

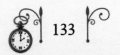

Atherton gave him a scornful look. "In a public house?" he said. "With all these witnesses? Really, old chap. I don't fancy your chances, do you?"

A look passed between Giles and Charlie, so quickly that Alex almost missed it.

"All right," Charlie said, after a pause. "I'll go and fetch it from the bus now, if you want."

"I should jolly well think so too!" said Mary. She turned to Atherton in triumph.

Atherton, very solemnly, took off his hat.

"You," he said in reverent tones, "are a queen among women. A goddess among mortals!"

"And don't you forget it," said Mary.

They trooped back out into the stable yard. Ruby

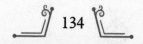

was standing by the roadside, making friends with a little boy on a pony. She looked round as they came out, obviously curious, but didn't come over. Giles leaned over to Charlie and murmured something, and Charlie nodded. Alex would have liked to warn Atherton, but Atherton was striding ahead, towards the car, and he wasn't sure exactly what it was he would have said anyway. His suspicions grew, however, as, passing Atherton's car, Giles stooped. Just for a moment.

"All right?" said Atherton, turning.

The valet, rising with a smoothness Jeeves would have been proud of, said, "Perfectly all right, sir."

They reached Charlie's little green open-topped

car. Charlie opened the side door, climbed in and felt under the seat.

Giles said, "If none of you objects, I'd better get the car started. Afraid the engine's a little temperamental."

Atherton brightened.

"I say, is it?" he said. "Mine was awfully tricky at first, but then d'you know what I did? I—"

Giles opened the bonnet and began doing something with a little can of what Alex supposed was petrol, while he and Atherton began a long, complicated discussion about engines and petrol and cold winter mornings.

Alex glanced worriedly at Mary who said, "Dearest, are you sure...?"

But Atherton didn't seem to hear.

Mary sighed, and said, "Come on, Charlie old man, buck up. Where's this Cup of yours then?"

"I know it's here somewhere..." said Charlie indistinctly, from underneath the seat.

The car engine gave a sputter and roared into life.

Atherton cried, "Oh, good show!" as Giles, looking pleased with himself, removed the starting handle and reattached the bonnet.

Mary said, "Now, look here. I don't know what you two think you're playing at, but—"

"Here," said Giles to Charlie. "You'd better let me do that."

He climbed into the car. Then, so quickly that

137

Alex barely had time to blink, he put the car into gear, swerved around Atherton, who leapt aside, and drove away in a flurry of dust, leaving them staring.

"Hey!" Alex yelled.

"That filthy toad!" Mary cried. "After him!"

Alex shouted, "No, wait!"

But Mary and Atherton were running back to the car.

"He's done something to the car!" Alex shouted. "That valet – I know he has!"

Atherton was already feeling the back tyre.

"Punctured!" he said. "The wart! The weasel! The excrement on the sole of human existence! Is there another—" He looked wildly around the yard, as though hoping for another car in which to give chase, but of course there were none. "Curse him!" he cried. "A curse on the house of Higgins and all their descendants! By the time we get there it'll all be fixed, of course. The Cup nicely back where it belongs, and only his word against mine! Curse and confound and discombobulate him!"

"Is something the matter?" said Ruby, wandering up. She looked rather pleased with herself.

"He's taken my Cup!" Atherton howled. "My beautiful Cup!"

"Your Cup?" said Ruby.

"Yes! My beautiful, beautiful Newberry Cup!"

"Oh," said Ruby. She opened her bag and pulled

out a large bundle wrapped in green velvet. "You mean this Cup?"

The four of them sat in a row on top of the gate, drinking lemonade (Mary and the children) and beer (Atherton) and waiting for the policemen.

"I don't suppose we'll have any more trouble from Charlie," Atherton said, waving his pipe in an expansive manner. "Never had much pluck, did Charlie. Although," he scratched his ear thoughtfully, "I might drop a line to his father, just to be on the safe side. Wonderful man, Mr Higgins. Probably polite to warn the old chap, before his artefact starts touring the country. And of course, if he wants the Cup back, we'll have to pony it up. It does belong to him, after all. But I suspect he'll just be grateful his son found a way to pay his debts like a gentleman."

He took a gulp of his ale.

Mary said, "No need to be so jolly smug about it. But what in heaven's name are you going to tell the police?"

"Oh, I think we'll tell them the truth, don't you? Might be as well to have them on our side. It's all right. I won't press charges. And if Charlie knows what's good for him, he won't do anything that means I have to."

And that seemed to be that. Except...

"We haven't actually seen the Cup yet," said Alex. "Well – I haven't, anyway. Ruby probably did when she rescued it."

"Not really," said Ruby. "I just peeped in to

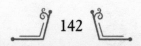

142

make sure. I didn't want you lot coming out and catching me with it. Can we? Given as how it was us who solved the crime and everything."

Atherton glanced at her. "I don't see why not," he said. "Sling it over, Mary."

The Cup was in Mary's handbag. Carefully, as though afraid she might break something, she lifted it out and unfolded the green velvet.

And inside was the Newberry Cup.

It was about the size of Mary's hand, with the fingers outstretched, an intricate Saxon chalice made of soft old gold and jewels. The outer sides of the Cup were engraved with complicated twining scrollwork, set with rubies and sapphires and emeralds.

It sparkled in the late afternoon sunlight, and it glowed a dull gold.

"Roman gold," said Atherton.

"It's beautiful," said Ruby, who never usually cared for anything like that at all.

"It's over a thousand years old," said Mary. "It was made for a Saxon lady, as a wedding gift for her chapel."

She looked up and her eyes met Atherton's, and suddenly Alex felt ashamed of watching, as though he were intruding on something private, and rather holy.

"Fitting that we bring it home today then," said Atherton, and his voice, for once, had no laughter in it. He put down his pipe and took her hand.

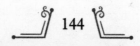

Mary lifted her face to his and stared, and then, for no reason that Alex could see, she blushed and looked away. Atherton grinned.

"What ho!" he said, and kissed her.

Eventually the police arrived, rather sweetly, on bicycles, and all the explanations had to be gone through again. The policemen seemed to share Atherton's view of things.

"Let's not go making more trouble than we have to," the inspector said. He shook his head. "Although I don't know what your brother will say about those stables."

Applecott House, when they finally made it back home, was full of wedding guests, noisy and cheerful and hungry for dinner. Mostly Pilgrims, but also relations of Mary's, and Mary's anthropologist friends, who were cheerful young women with names like Bunty and Cyril, and Atherton's friends from Cambridge, who were cheerful young men with names like Algy and Guffy. Everyone was very enthusiastic about their adventures with the Newberry Cup, and there was a general feeling that catching robbers was just the sort of jolly good thing that jolly good sorts like Atherton and Mary would do. Alex and Ruby found it rather bewildering. They were sure their own parents would have been more surprised. (The eldest brother, Uncle Edmund, shook his head and looked disapproving, then went off to talk about interest rates with the vicar in the corner.)

There was an awful lot of explaining to do. Alex and Ruby were formally introduced to Dora and Henry's parents, who one apparently had to refer to as Mr and Mrs Pilgrim, like teachers. Dora's father was a historian. Alex was pretty sure that in modern Britain, historians taught in universities or schools or something, but Dora's father seemed to just stay at home and look after the house and write monographs on ancient kings and queens. He was very excited about the Newberry Cup, and he and Atherton immediately started a long and complicated discussion about King Alfred, and Rædwald, and all sorts of people Alex had never heard of. Alex found it strangely exciting. All the grown-ups he knew in the future had boring, sensible jobs like being teachers, or plumbers, or working in offices. These people who charged about the world finding things out and having ideas and discovering things were a whole other breed. He watched the brothers talking, and wondered if one could live a life like that in the twenty-first century. He was a Pilgrim, just like they were. If they could do it, could he?

He was still wondering when he felt Ruby at his elbow.

"Come *on*," she said. "The mirror. While they're all talking. Let's see if it'll let us go home."

They slipped out of the living room, into the

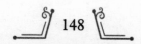

hall. The mirror was showing the 1912 hallway. Alex's heart sank. Ruby, however, marched right up to it.

"Come on then," she said. "We got your stupid Cup back. It's your turn now. Take us home."

"Ruby—" said Alex.

"Shut up!" said Ruby. She pressed her finger against the glass. "We can't stay here forever!" she said accusingly. "We've got people waiting for us! Parents! Lives! Send us back! Right now!"

But the mirror did not change. It stayed looking exactly as it had before, innocently reflecting the 1912 hallway: the table, the green plant and the door.

Ruby was in shock.

"Where are we going to sleep?" she said to Dora and Alex. "Where are we going to *live*? We can't stay here forever!"

"You can stay tonight," said Dora. "Don't fuss. Everyone will think you're a distant cousin, or you belong to a friend of Miss Flynn's or something. After the wedding... We'll work something out. I promise."

Alex was pretty sure that his parents would have noticed two strangers descending on their house, even if they had as many people staying the night as the Pilgrims seemed to. But Dora was quite right. All of the bedrooms were taken, but Dora and Henry and various other children would be

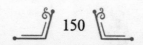

sleeping on straw-filled mattresses in the drawing room, and nobody seemed to mind that Alex and Ruby would be sleeping there too.

Ruby's lips were pressed together in silence. Alex knew he ought to be worried too, but somehow he felt sure that the mirror – *his* mirror – wouldn't abandon them in 1912. And soon Henry was banging the gong and calling them in for a busy, cheerful, rather chaotic dinner in the dining room, and there were all sorts of mysterious foods to be investigated, like "shape", and suet pudding, and tongue, which was an actual cow's tongue, fried and cut into slices, and soda water, which came in a siphon, and then one of Mary's friends discovered the piano and began to play a dancing tune, and Dora's father discovered an accordion and joined in, and suddenly everyone was singing.

"You're enjoying yourself," Ruby said, just as Mary had said to Atherton. And Alex realised she was right. He was.

CHAPTER NINE
GHOSTS IN THE GLASS

The next day was the wedding.

The wedding was held in the village church at Dalton, which was small and cool, with devil's faces painted on the ends of the beams, and dark wood pews with embroidered footrests hanging from their backs. Alex and Ruby had actually been to another Pilgrim wedding in exactly the same church – and probably, they thought, that bride was a descendant of one of the people here. (They still hadn't figured out which of the three Pilgrim brothers was their however-many-greats-grandfather, although they supposed it must be one of them). The expectant feel in the church was just the same, once you got used to the clothes being different. Ruby was wearing a white muslin party dress of Dora's, which she said made her look about six. Alex had got away more lightly with a grey suit that wasn't too different to the one he'd worn to Auntie Debbie's wedding, if you overlooked the stockings and the knickerbockers and the detachable collar.

Mary looked most unlike herself in a white dress. Atherton looked exactly like himself in a morning coat and top hat. He was beaming so hard when Mary came down the aisle that several members of the congregation started beaming too, in sympathy.

Afterwards, there was rice-throwing and photographs outside the church. And then the whole wedding party went to the church hall for scones, and cake, and little triangular sandwiches handed round on trays by girls from the village.

"See!" said Alex to Ruby. "You *did* get cucumber sandwiches after all!"

"Huh," said Ruby. "Is this all the food we get?

At least in modern times there's a proper meal."

There was a telegraph boy on a red bicycle who kept knocking on the door with telegrams for the

bride and groom. There was a display of all the presents on a table. (At Auntie Debbie's wedding there'd been a table for presents too, but all of *her* presents had been wrapped.) It was very funny seeing what people had thought Atherton and Mary might want to sustain them in their married life. A silver-plated biscuit barrel. A silver fish slice. A little framed cross-stitch motto that read *God is Love*, with cross-stitch lilies underneath it. There were some rather peculiar presents too: one of Mary's anthropologist friends contributed a fertility doll from Papua New Guinea, and one of Atherton's university friends gave a pair of garden gnomes as a joke.

Alex and Ruby's parents had bought Auntie

Debbie an ice-cream maker. Alex wondered if she'd used it any more than Atherton would his silver fish slice.

The best man made a very funny speech and read out all the telegrams. Then there was champagne and wedding cake, which was *just* the same as at Auntie Debbie's wedding.

While everyone was eating their wedding cake, Atherton and Mary disappeared, then reappeared at the doorway, waving. They'd changed out of their wedding finery and were dressed in more normal – but still nice – clothes.

"What are they doing?" said Ruby.

"They're going on honeymoon," said Dora. "They're going to Egypt, only not straight away;

tonight they're just going to Southampton. Don't you think Mary's going-away dress is awfully nice?"

"They're going on honeymoon already?" said Ruby. "But we haven't had the dancing!"

There was definitely going to be dancing. There was a band getting ready in the corner of the hall.

Dora stared.

"You don't dance at your own *wedding*!" she said.

"Why not?" said Ruby. "You do in the future!"

But you didn't in the past, apparently. There was waving, and hugging, and exclamations, and then Atherton and Mary were driving away, and the band were striking up, and it was time to dance.

The dancing at Auntie Debbie's wedding had meant a DJ and disco lights. This dancing, however, had rules. All of the dances had names – polkas, and tangos, and waltzes – and they all had to be done in different ways. Even children were expected to know what to do, and even little children like Henry apparently did. (Alex supposed that was what one learned at the white-socked dancing class.)

"Aren't you going to dance?" said Henry.

"No. Way." said Ruby. She looked horrified.

Alex was rather wistful; he'd liked the dancing at Auntie Debbie's wedding.

"This one's a waltz," said Dora. "Anyone can waltz, come on." And she put her arm around him and showed him.

"Like it?" she said, smiling at him with a rather superior grown-up sort of smile.

"I like our dancing better," said Alex.

The four of them went out into the porch, where the music could still be heard but no one could see them. Dora was in the middle of explaining how a polka worked, when a head appeared around the door. It was Atherton.

"We thought you'd gone ages ago!" Dora cried.

"Sorting some things out," he said briefly. "We were just about to head off and I thought... Well. Knowing Mary and I, we'll probably get kidnapped by grave robbers or something. Someone sensible ought to know where our Cup is." He jerked his head towards the door. "Want to come and see how the story ends?"

The village was quiet as they walked back to the house. Applecott House was silent and empty. The only light came from the hall, where Mary was standing in front of the mirror, the Newberry Cup under her arm. She turned as Atherton and the children came in, and smiled.

"I've been admiring my wedding present," she said.

Alex came and stood beside her. The mirror looked even more mysterious than usual, there in the twilight.

"It's old," said Alex. "Isn't it?"

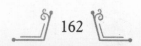

"Eighteenth century," said Atherton. "They say that it belonged to a French countess. A woman called Jeanne d'Allonette. She was believed by some to be a witch." He traced his fingers across the frame. "It belonged to my grandmother. One of my ancestors brought it back from France after the revolution. My grandmother said that during the French Revolution, the revolutionaries came to arrest Jeanne and her child. You understand – if they had been caught, they would have been executed. Jeanne locked herself and her son in her dressing room. When the revolutionaries managed to break down the door, they found the room was empty – except for this mirror, which showed another room in another place. The men said it was witchcraft and tried to smash the mirror, but they found it would not break."

"And what happened to the countess?" said Ruby.

"She was never seen again," said Atherton. He glanced at Alex. "They say that this mirror is haunted by ghosts. But my grandmother also said it is considered a lucky object." He patted the glass. "That's why I gave it to Mary, you see – we like a bit of witchcraft, Mary and I, in moderation, and I thought it might be helpful to have a few friendly ghosts watching over her." Again, that look at Alex. "It turns out I was right."

Henry said fiercely, "They aren't *ghosts*! They're *time travellers*."

Atherton dropped his hand and laughed.

"Well," he said. "Perhaps that's the same thing."

"And the bottle?" said Alex. "There was a bottle. Silver. About this big. I opened it, and…" He stopped. Making a wish on a genie seemed like a foolish thing to admit to.

Dora said, "Oh, it's the witch in the bottle!"

"So it is!" said Atherton.

"That's not Uncle Atherton's," said Dora. "It's older than that. Grandfather got it from a woman in the village. She said there'd be trouble if we ever opened it."

"She was right," Ruby muttered.

Alex didn't quite know what to say to that, so he changed the subject.

"What are you going to do with the Newberry Cup?" he said.

"Ah," said Atherton. "Yes. Come with me."

He took the Cup, tucked it under his arm, and led Mary and the children back into the drawing room. Ruby raised her eyebrows at Dora, but she shrugged.

In the drawing room, Atherton turned on the electric light and went straight to the corner. He tugged on the bookcase that stood in front of it.

"Take the other end for me, would you, dearest?" he said, a little breathlessly. Mary obeyed. The amused expression was back.

"Whatever *are* you doing?" she said.

Atherton pulled the case aside and knelt down

166

on the floor. The walls of this room were covered in old-fashioned wooden panels – wainscotting, it was called, Alex knew. Mary and the children crowded around him.

He felt with his long fingers at the edge of the panelling. No one spoke, not even Henry. There was a breathless air of expectation, and then, suddenly: *click*.

The panel slid back and aside, like a compartment on a puzzle box. Behind it was a dark hole.

"Whoa!" said Ruby. "Cool!"

"It's a secret compartment!" said Dora. "Why didn't we know about it?"

"I don't think even Edmund knows about it," said Atherton. "I found it when I was a little

boy playing smugglers. I used to hide marbles and soldiers and things in it. I always wanted something really valuable to keep in here."

"But, darling," said Mary. "Is it really secure? Wouldn't a bank vault be safer?"

"I don't think you could find many places in all of England more secure than this," said Atherton. "I believe I'm the only person in the family who knows about it – besides you lovely people, of course. There were simply acres of dust in here when I opened it. I don't believe it had been touched in hundreds of years."

He took the bundle and laid it carefully in the hole in the wall.

"But – are you sure you want us to know about

it?" Alex said awkwardly. "Ruby and me, I mean. You hardly know us."

"No," said Atherton. He gave Alex a curious look. "I don't, do I?" He slid the panel back and it shut with a *click*. "Perhaps I ought to find out who you really are ... but I'm not sure I want to. Some things are best left a mystery."

The dancing was still going on in the hall, but Dora and Henry's mother appeared to hurry them into bed. Alex supposed they ought to go too; the longer they stayed, the more likely it was that someone would notice them and start asking questions. All of the other cousins were busy preparing for bed; the living room was full of wails over lost possessions and protestations over lumpy mattresses.

Henry was insisting that he "wasn't *a bit* sleepy!" much to the irritation of his mother, a lively woman who looked rather like a grown-up Dora.

Alex stood in the doorway looking out at the garden. Night was falling, a deep-blue, rather lovely twilight. There was a full moon over the cornfields behind the house, and choirs upon choirs of birds singing to the evening in the garden trees. He could faintly hear the sound of music coming from the hall. He breathed in, savouring the memory.

When he turned, he wasn't at all surprised to

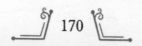

see that the mirror showed the hallway at Aunt Joanna's house. It was evening, just as it had been evening when he and Ruby had left.

"Ruby," he called cautiously, not wanting to draw attention to what was happening.

Ruby appeared in the doorway of the drawing room. She gasped when she saw the mirror.

"Quick!" she said, but Alex shook his head.

"Clothes," he said. "You can't go back looking like that!"

"But what if the mirror closes?" she said.

Alex shook his head again. "It won't." He wasn't sure why he was so certain, but he was.

Ruby bolted up the stairs to Dora's room. Alex followed, more slowly. Ruby was changing at

lightning speed, pulling off her layers of 1912 underclothes. Alex, rather reluctantly, did the same. Now that the time had come to go, he didn't want to leave.

"Oh, hurry!" said Ruby. "We don't want to be left behind!" She tugged on her shoes and ran down the stairs. Alex shrugged on his T-shirt, picked up his trainers and followed her.

The mirror was hanging against the wall, looking exactly as they'd left it. Ruby had stopped in front of it, looking suddenly uncertain.

"Hold my hand?" she said. "I don't want you to get left behind."

"I won't," said Alex.

"I know," said Ruby. "But ... just to be sure?"

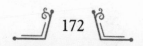

She seemed wary. And, Alex thought suddenly, why shouldn't she? Who knew what they would find on the other side of the mirror. Perhaps they'd been gone for weeks and weeks. Perhaps that wasn't Aunt Joanna's hallway at all. Perhaps, just by being here, they'd changed history so much that when they got home, everything would be different.

He took her hand.

"Ready?" she said. He nodded.

"Ready."

And they stepped through the looking glass together.

CHAPTER TEN
WHAT HAPPENED TO THE CUP

Alex tumbled forward and landed on his stomach. For a moment he lay breathless and rather dizzy. Beside him, he could hear Ruby making *aargh* and *ow* noises, but he ignored her. He sat up slowly and looked around. Cream walls. Brown door. A copy of the *Radio Times*, Alex's blue jumper, and a leaflet advertising a pizza delivery company on the hall table.

"Home!" said Ruby in triumph.

Home.

"How long do you think we've been away?" Ruby said, sitting up. "Do you reckon that mirror works on Narnia time? I do. Otherwise there'd be policemen and film crews and weeping parents and all sorts, wouldn't there? Shall we find out? Aunt Joanna! We're home! Cancel the funeral!"

She scrambled upright and headed off in the direction of the living room. Alex bent and put on his trainers, then followed slowly. Even the very familiarity of the house was strange. The brightness of the twenty-first-century lights. The radiators. The colour photographs on the sideboard. He felt like he'd been away for years and years and years.

Ruby was standing in the living room doorway, talking to Aunt Joanna, who didn't look at all surprised to see them.

"... and *then*," Ruby was saying, "we found ourselves back here! Like nothing had happened!"

"Goodness!" said Aunt Joanna. "Did you remember to clean your teeth, in between saving the family fortune?"

Normally, Alex knew, Ruby would be insulted by the mere suggestion that she'd been playing make-believe games. But today there were more

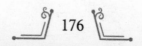

important things to think about.

"See!" she said, turning to Alex. "Narnia time! But, Aunt Joanna, we can *prove* it. We met loads of old Pilgrims. Atherton, and Mary, and Dora, and Henry, and – what was their dad called?"

"Oswald," said Alex. "And the other one was Edmund."

"That's right," said Aunt Joanna. "Edmund was my grandfather. We had all their pictures out last year, didn't we? Or was it the year before? You *have* got a good memory."

"I don't remember being shown pictures *at all*," said Ruby crossly.

Aunt Joanna went over to the old-fashioned bookcase against the living room wall, the one with the glass doors that opened with little metal keys. Alex realised suddenly that Atherton and Mary and Dora and Henry must all be dead. Of course they must. They must have been dead for years.

He wasn't sure why he minded this quite so much.

Aunt Joanna took one of the old black family photograph albums out of the bookcase and started turning the pages, saying things like, "That's my brother Gordon, your grandfather. And that's my father as a baby – doesn't he look funny? And that's – oh, yes! There you are!"

It was a black-and-white studio portrait of a young man wearing a soldier's uniform and a soldier's cap and a neat little moustache, looking very solemn and distant and long ago. Alex stared at the photograph. It seemed incredible that only yesterday that same young man had been saying, "What ho!" and kissing his lady-love under the greenery. The man in the picture seemed to belong to a different time entirely.

"That's—" said Ruby.

"My Great-Uncle Atherton," said Aunt Joanna. "He was my grandfather's younger brother. I *must* have told you about him. He brought back half the furniture in this house from his travels. He was a great collector. He had some idea of exhibiting everything, I think but of course, the War put a stop to all that. He was killed in Gallipoli in 1915.

Do you know about the Gallipoli Campaign? It was what was called a *glorious disaster* – such a nonsense, of course, but at the time it was considered rather a noble thing to be involved in, like a last, desperate stand, you know."

Alex looked at Ruby. He was relieved to see that she too looked rather shaken. The young man in the grey flannel suit had only lived another three years after they'd seen him. It was a strange, sobering thought.

"And Mary?" he said.

"Oh yes." Aunt Joanna turned back a page. There was another studio portrait, Mary this time, surrounded by photographer's props – a velvet armchair and an empty birdcage – looking, like Atherton, very formal and long ago. "She was an administrator in a women's hospital in Egypt. Quite a remarkable woman, by all accounts. She was killed in the War too, when the liner she was travelling home on was torpedoed. They died within a few days of each other. My grandfather always hoped that Atherton never knew what had happened to her – but he always wondered, of course, if that was why—"

"He died of a broken heart," said Ruby solemnly.

"Well, no," said Aunt Joanna. "He was killed by the Turks. But, perhaps… Well, anyway! It was a long time ago, and not worth worrying about."

She meant, Alex knew, that perhaps Atherton had stopped caring whether he lived or died after

Mary was killed. He wondered if she was right. He thought of the young man in the top hat, beaming at Mary as she came down the aisle.

Like Uncle Edmund, Alex hoped he hadn't known.

"But what about Dora and Henry?" Ruby was saying. "What happened to them?"

"Oh, well." Now Aunt Joanna was smiling. "Uncle Oswald emigrated to New Zealand just before the War. He got a very important job at a university, teaching ancient British history. The whole family settled over there. Let me see…"

She put the photograph album back on the shelf and pulled out another, more recent, album. This time she found what she was looking for almost

immediately.

"There!" she said.

It was a picture of a family party, the sort that were always held at Applecott House. A small, white-haired woman sitting in a chair, a plate with cake on it on her lap. Alex was sure he had never seen her before, and yet...

"That was 1985," said Aunt Joanna. "Dora brought her family over from Christchurch to show her children the house where she'd grown up. She was eighty-six! Another remarkable woman. She had two children of her own, and four war orphans that she'd adopted. But then," and she smiled at Ruby, "Pilgrims always did live adventurous lives."

1985. Not really very long ago at all. Dora had grown up into a world with pop stars, and televisions, and aeroplanes to Christchurch. He wondered what she'd made of it all.

"But what happened to the Cup?" said Ruby.

"The Cup, dear?"

"The Newberry Cup!" said Ruby. "I *told* you. We rescued it from the robbers, and we hid it in the secret compartment in the drawing room, until Atherton could get his collection of antiquities together!"

"Goodness!" said Aunt Joanna in her what-a-lovely-game voice. "I was born in this house, and *I* never knew we had a secret compartment. How exciting!"

Alex and Ruby looked at each other.

"You don't think…?" said Alex.

"Come on," said Ruby. And she grabbed Aunt Joanna's arm and dragged her out of the living room and across the hall to the drawing room.

Dora and Henry's drawing room, in Aunt Joanna's house, was given over to the bed-and-breakfast guests as a sitting room. There were two of them in there now, an elderly couple reading on the sofa. They looked up in mild annoyance as Ruby barged through the door and over to the corner.

"S'cuse me, s'cuse me, terribly sorry, terribly important secret panel discovery work going on here, *thank* you."

"Ruby, dear, is now the time…?" said Aunt Joanna.

Ruby and Alex ignored her. They were too busy pulling the armchair away from the corner. Ruby hopped down on to her knees and began pushing at bits of the wooden panelling with more optimism than success.

Alex said impatiently, "Let *me*."

He crouched down and felt around for the place Atherton had shown him, a few minutes and over a hundred years ago. He found it easily and pushed. It was rather stiff, but it *did* push. The

panel moved.

"Good heavens!" said one of the bed-and-breakfast guests.

Aunt Joanna said, "Alex! However did you find that?"

Ruby, always impatient, yanked on the panel.

Alex said, "Be careful! It probably hasn't been opened in a hundred years."

"I bet it jolly well hasn't!" said Ruby, and began to giggle rather hysterically.

Alex ignored her and slid the panel aside. Inside, the little hole was dark and cobwebby.

Alex reached in. There *was* something there. Something bulky and heavy and covered in spiders' webs, and wrapped in dark cloth.

It was the Newberry Cup.

It was very much later. The children had been put to bed, the bed-and-breakfast guests had stopped exclaiming excitedly, and Aunt Joanna's antique dealer friend in Cambridge – with whom she had been organising the sale of most of the furniture – had finally stopped calling Aunt Joanna back about the Newberry Cup. The antique dealer was a musty, fussy sort of person, who never said "Ooh!" without adding a "But…" Aunt Joanna had never seen him anywhere near as excited as he'd sounded when Ruby had sent him the pictures of the Newberry Cup. It was only with great difficulty that she'd prevented him from getting into his car and driving to Applecott House that very night. He was coming tomorrow morning with several expert friends of his to examine the Cup properly, but if it was genuine – and he seemed to think that it was – it was clear that Aunt Joanna would never have to worry about money ever again.

It was all a little bewildering.

Aunt Joanna sat in the living room with a cat on her lap, and a glass of Madeira, and tried to make sense of it. She still wasn't sure how the children had found that compartment. She supposed they must have been playing at detectives, and pressed the secret place on the panel by mistake – although she would have thought they'd be getting too old for that sort of game. Of course, they must have remembered the family names from the photograph albums. Or perhaps their parents had been telling them stories. Either way, it was most unlike them.

The photograph albums... There was something worrying Aunt Joanna about the photograph albums. Something half remembered. Something that didn't quite fit with this very logical view of the affair.

She put down her glass of Madeira and went over to the bookcase. Which album was it again? This one? No, this. She turned the pages until she came to the picture she wanted. *Ah*.

A group portrait. A wedding picture, taken outside the little village church. *Atherton Pilgrim and Mary Flynn, August 1912*, read the caption. The bride and groom stood in the centre of the picture, wearing rather stiff smiles, surrounded by wedding guests in all their Edwardian finery. Aunt Joanna had never paid much attention to the picture before. But she was almost sure...

At the edge of the photograph, half hidden behind the other guests, a boy and a girl. The girl's face was half in shadow, and the boy, rather inconveniently, was looking to the side. And of course, these old photographs... But still. The resemblance was rather disconcerting.

Aunt Joanna gave herself a mental shake. Family resemblances *were* peculiar things. Of course, the children in the picture must be distant Pilgrim cousins, although right now she couldn't put her finger on which ones exactly. It wasn't so surprising that they should look like her great-niece and great-nephew, was it?

It didn't mean their story was *real*.

She closed the photograph album firmly and put it back on the shelf. Time for bed.

The hall was quiet, with the peculiar stillness of a sleeping house. Aunt Joanna stopped by the long mirror against the wall. Her own reflection frowned back at her. She was getting old. She had been getting old for a long time now.

There had always been strange stories about that mirror. Something about a witch, wasn't it? Or a French countess? Or a countess who was a witch? You would have thought a story like that would be frightening, but Aunt Joanna could never be frightened of the mirror, even as a child.

She shook her head. She was too old to be thinking about fairy tales. As she turned away to go upstairs, the reflection in the mirror changed. Now it showed a hallway all decked out as though for Christmas. There was a wreath of holly on the back of the front door, and a great ball of mistletoe hanging from the ceiling, and old-fashioned-looking Christmas cards on strings on the walls. Outside the windows the world was dark, and in

the hallway, gaslights flickered in their sconces. Brown-paper packages were piled up under the umbrella stand, as though abandoned there after a shopping trip, and there was a muddy, friendly clutter of boots and hats and hoops and skates and cricket bats under the coat rack, as though the house was living in by a whole pack of cheerful, untidy children.

As though to confirm this guess, a little girl with thick black hair, dressed rather like Alice in Wonderland in an old-fashioned dress and white apron, came charging past the mirror at full pelt. She was followed by a boy in a knickerbocker suit, then another, and another – how many were there – three, four, five? They went past so quickly, it was impossible to count. And then, behind them, walking slowly, head down, a little girl dressed all in black: black dress, black boots, black stockings, even a black ribbon in her thin, fair hair. She didn't glance at the mirror, just trudged past and was gone.

The picture rippled. Now it showed the twenty-first-century hallway, just as it always did. But something in the movement had caught Aunt Joanna's eye, and she turned. Was there something there?

No. No, there was nothing. Just the familiar, sleeping hallway. Of course. Of course.

Such foolishness, Aunt Joanna thought to herself, and climbed the stairs to bed.

TAKE ANOTHER TRIP THROUGH TIME WITH ALEX AND RUBY!

A CHRISTMAS IN TIME

CHAPTER ONE
CHRISTMAS WITH
AUNT JOANNA

Christmas at Applecott House was the busiest time of year. Aunt Joanna organised a whole three-day celebration for her bed-and-breakfast guests, with a carol service in the village, a musical evening in the drawing room, and a Boxing

Day quiz. There was fizzy wine with Christmas breakfast, and candlelit dinners on Christmas Eve and Christmas Day, which Aunt Joanna had to cook. Alex privately agreed with Ruby that it didn't really sound like *Christmas* at all, but lots of grown-ups seemed to like it, and she was always booked out months in advance.

And now it looked like she would have to cancel.

Aunt Joanna had called the children's father in a panic. All of the food and wine was ordered already. She'd paid a deposit for the wine glasses and the musicians. Everyone was relying on her. She couldn't ask her own children to help (Aunt Joanna had a son who lived in Australia and a daughter who had baby twins, and obviously neither could be expected to drop everything and run Christmas in Applecott House). But perhaps Alex's family might be able to…

"There won't be any beds," said Alex's father. "All the rooms are booked, so we'll be sleeping in the living room, I'm afraid. Aunt Joanna thinks she should be able to supervise the cooking – at least I hope will, because you know what our cooking's like, and Stacey will be in as much as she can." Stacey was a woman from the village who helped Aunt Joanna out at busy times of year. "It's mostly getting the rooms ready … and the washing up, and the vegetable-chopping … and the decorations – apparently that's very important. And I suppose there'll be lots of tidying up and laying tables and so on. But she's been so good to us over the years – I don't know what we'd have done if she hadn't agreed to look after you children. And... Well. I didn't really feel I could say no. And it's supposed to be rather a luxury holiday ... I understand people pay a fortune, and of course we'd get to eat all the food and so forth. I think it might be quite fun, really..."

"But it's Christmas!" Ruby had said. "Christmas Day!"

"I don't imagine you children will have to help too much on Christmas Day itself," their mother said hurriedly. (Alex got the impression she wasn't keen on spending Christmas laying tables and loading dishwashers either.) "I expect you'll be able to hide somewhere with your presents if you'd rather."

"I don't see where," Ruby muttered. "We won't even have a *bedroom*."

But Alex didn't really mind. Just being back at Applecott House – his favourite place in all the world – was enough to make him happy. They'd arrived yesterday, just after lunch, and even an afternoon spent making beds and vacuuming bedrooms had been fun. He'd enjoyed hanging up all the decorations, and helping Aunt Joanna ice Christmas biscuits. He was looking forward to eating all this fancy food – and after all, he thought, their father was right. Aunt Joanna was *family*.

"We're hardly going to see Mum and Dad all Christmas!" said Ruby furiously. "They're going to spend all day washing dishes and chopping carrots, just you wait. It's going to be awful! I wish we were *anywhere* else. I wish we could just *leave* and go and have a *proper* Christmas. Anywhere!"

She swung away from the window to glare at Alex. And stiffened.

"Alex!"

"I know," said Alex, who'd seen it too. "I think you might be about to get your wish."

He hurried over to the wall, Ruby close on his heels. The mirror – the magic mirror, the time-travelling mirror, *their* mirror – now showed a middle-aged woman in a very old-fashioned dress

– Victorian, probably, Alex thought – with a woollen shawl and big old-fashioned skirts. She was frowning at her reflection in the mirror, a hatpin poised above her hat. Then suddenly something changed. A look of astonishment passed over her face, as  though she couldn't believe what she was seeing. She took a step backwards, staring at the mirror as though it was a ghost.

"She can see us!" cried Ruby. She grabbed his

hand. "I didn't know that could happen."

The woman blinked, and rubbed her eyes. She took a deep breath. And then slowly, cautiously, arm outstretched, she began to move towards the mirror.

"No!" Ruby cried. "If she touches it, she's going to come *here*. No way, old Victorian lady. This is *our* time-travelling adventure, not yours!"

She pulled Alex forwards, into the mirror...